FROM R.L. BUSS

Life Between Cigarettes	*1996*
I Threw a Cookie at Eddie Vedder	*1997*
Goodnight My Jellybye Baby	*2005*
Spread Out Across the Lowering Sky	*2006*

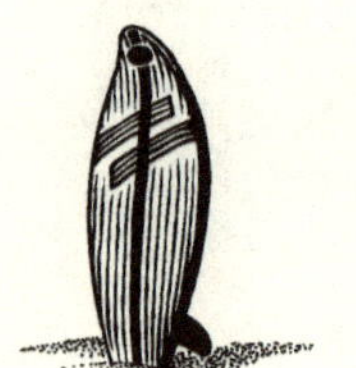

SUSPICION OF INDIFFERENCE

R.L. BUSS

RAGGED ARCHETYPES CHICAGO 2015

Suspicion of Indifference

ISBN: 978-0-9713360-5-6

FIRST EDITION

for America's cool dusk…

Look for the ridiculous in everything
and you will find it.

JULES RENARD

There is nothing so powerful as truth
and often nothing so strange.

DANIEL WEBSTER

Los Palaveres, Southern California

1999

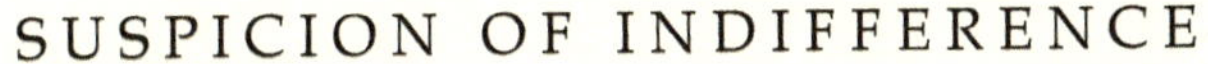

SUSPICION OF INDIFFERENCE

Rap 1

I WAS THIRTY YEARS OLD. I smoked pot every day. I drank beer almost every day. I was living in an old friend's garage. I was a professional pornographic letter writer. I had three letters to fire off to different editors, and checks to write for past due bills. My car was about to break down. Only the sad songs made me horny.

The monument to all this stood on the front lawn. It was a surfboard. It was neatly trimmed in shape, and a crack from some mishap ran down its spine. The surfboard's owner had planted it to stand for all time. It was orange and yellow. It had one fin. Plants had grown up around it. In the morning, if there was no fog, the board would cast a shadow across the dewey grass that was cool if you walked through it with bare feet. It was there in the shadow I woke up that morning.

I stood up, looked around. There was a strange lady watering her lawn with a green garden hose. She cut her eyes at me and moved cautiously toward her house. The front of my clothing was all wet from the dew as I had been resting face down in the grass. A man was bringing his trash out to the curb. I made a move for my front door and he became startled.

"Goddamn," he said, "I didn't see you there." I wanted to

say something but I puked on the sidewalk in front of my doorstep. "Goddamn, buddy," he said, "you're, like, way fucked up."

I finally stumbled to the door but it was locked. I fumbled for my key but couldn't find it. I would have to jump the fence. I rounded the corner of the house by the garage where I usually jumped over. I could hear music from inside the garage. I banged on the door. Nobody answered. I vaulted over the fence.

Suddenly I was face to face with Tipsy Russell, my roommate's English Mastiff who apparently didn't recognize me. He immediately had me on the ground with his jaws locked in a grip around my throat.

"Tips! You beast!" The dog answered the call of Jack, my housemate, friend and Tipsy's master. "Come here, boy!"

He released his death grip. My heart was beating fast and breath was steaming out of my mouth. I stayed on the ground for about twenty minutes. The dirt felt good. It was cool and dry. I told myself I would get up when the shadow of the fence reached my head. It was getting close. Soon my face would be in the sunlight. I wanted to beat the sun by rising just before it had a chance to shine in my eyes.

There was a parrot circling overhead. I could hear the neighbors leaving for work, slamming doors and starting cars. I was almost lonely waiting for the sun. I wanted Tipsy to come back and lick my face. I could hear the sound of the freeway. There was mad laughter from inside the garage to go with the music.

I fell asleep.

Rap 2

I WOKE TO DISCOVER more than twenty minutes had passed. My face was sun burnt and my head was throbbing. It was early afternoon and our neighbors were having a party in the yard across the alley. The music was loud. I got up and went into the garage.

There were two young, desert-skinned girls, about eighteen years old asleep on my bed. They looked familiar. Someone was cooking fajita meat in the kitchen. The odor of flesh being seared made me sick. I leaned over and vomited into the washing machine. When I was through I started the wash cycle, heavy duty soil. One of the girls on my bed turned over and wrapped her leg around the waist of the other girl. I could hear the beef sizzling in the frying pan in the other room. I was dehydrated and needed some liquid.

The kitchen was filled with smoke. Jack was the one making fajitas.

"You fell asleep in the backyard, dude," he said.

"Yes, I know," I said.

"There's a paper in the living room," he said, shutting off the stove. I poured a glass of tap water and went into the living room. It was quiet there, and cool. At last I could relax. I sat on the couch. There was a breeze blowing in the front door. It felt refreshing.

I always read the front page. The first thing I saw was the picture of a young woman being loaded into a helicopter on a stretcher. The headline over the photo read: "Woman Mauled By Rabid Mountain Lion." I folded the paper neatly in half and set it on the couch next to me. Through the back door I could hear the party across the alley. I sipped the water and closed my eyes.

Rap 3

ALMOST IMMEDIATELY SOMEONE WAS KNOCKING on the screen door. I ignored them. Jack or someone else would answer it. The banging persisted. I opened my eyes a crack. The actual front door was always left open. I could make out a figure peering through the metal screen. She looked familiar. She noticed me on the couch.

"Dammit, Mudd," she said, "wake your goddamn lazy ass up! Wake up!"

I ignored her. She began pounding on the metal screen.

"I know you can hear me you bastard! Why didn't you call me last night?" She pounded again. "You said you would!"

I recognized the voice now. It was my girlfriend, Veronica. I ignored her.

"Fuck you, Mudd! I know you can hear me." She was cupping her hands to reduce the glare from the sun. Her jewelry rattled each time she hit the door. She always wore a lot of bracelets and rings. I could not avoid her much longer. I opened my eyes.

"Who is it?" I asked.

"You know who the fuck this is, you asshole. Now, unlock this door and let me in!" The dogs across the street were barking now.

"Hang on," I said, reaching for a pack of cigarettes on the coffee table. It was empty so I pulled a substantial butt from the ashtray and lit it. I sat there for about a minute.

"It's about goddamn time," she said when I opened the door. She came in, and I sat back down on the couch and closed my eyes. She climbed on top of me.

"Baby, you know I miss you when you don't call." She began kissing me on the neck. Veronica was a very forgiving woman. If I failed to call her for a period of time it made her want me more. I cannot explain it. That's just the way she was.

"Let's go in on your bed," she said, running her hands over my chest. She saw through me. She knew I was weak. I opened my eyes.

"I have a headache," I said. Which was true. Veronica began kissing my head.

"I've got the cure for your headache." She was treating me like a little boy. "You're all red. Did you fall asleep in the yard again?" She got up and grabbed my hand. "C'mon, let's go lay down on your bed."

My dick was now hard enough for mashed potatoes, and I looked down to make sure it wasn't obvious. Veronica was pulling on my arms. She wanted to screw. The front of my shirt and jeans was covered in dried grass clippings.

"I can't do anything looking like this," I said.

"You'll be out of those clothes in no time." She was

pulling hard now.

Then I remembered. There were two teenage girls in my bed.

"Let's go have a cigarette first," I said.

"You just had one." She was pulling me toward the garage. I couldn't stop her. We were almost to my door.

"So what did you do last night, dear?" I asked.

"I stayed at home and thought about you," she said.

As she reached for the knob the door opened. One of the desert-skinned girls, the one who had stretched her leg over the other, stepped out wearing one of my t-shirts. It was a t-shirt that Veronica had given me for my twenty-ninth birthday. It had been special ordered and embroidered with the words: "Veronica's Cock." The phone rang.

"I'll get it," I said. Veronica beat me to it.

"Hello...yes," she said, then looked at me. I grabbed for the phone. She was too quick. "No, he's not here right now." Then she hung up. I turned around and she ripped the phone out of the wall and threw it at the back of my head. It rang when it hit my head and it rang when it hit the floor.

"You bastard!" she screamed. "Man-cunt!" She slapped the back of my head. "I oughta cut off your motherfuckin' dick, you whore! Fucking cheap-ass gigolo!" Then she hissed like a cat at the girl and flipped her the bird. When Veronica slammed the door on her way out one of Jack's framed pictures fell off the wall.

My head didn't hurt anymore. I stood and looked at the floor for a minute. Then I looked up at the girl in my t-shirt. She was standing with one leg feeling its way up the corner of the wall. We went back to my bed. I fell asleep between them. I still couldn't figure out who the hell they were.

Rap 4

IT WAS AT LEAST THREE DAYS before I could face my neighbors again. They kept their eyes on me. They didn't leave their yards. I didn't say anything. I just got in my car and drove off.

It was going to be a good day, I thought. I was getting back together with Veronica. I was on my way to eat dinner with her, fresh fish tacos. I was wearing my best sport coat. I listened to a big band station on the way across town to her place. The sport coat had an inside pocket large enough to fit a pint of gin. I sipped from the bottle as I drove.

Veronica shared a house on the side of a cliff. It was very steep. My car often reached her driveway with great reluctance. That day was no different. By the time I got to the top near the driveway my transmission locked up. I could go no further. I was so close I could see her house. The car began to roll backwards down the hill. I stepped on the foot brake but nothing happened. I could only steer and use the emergency brake. Cars honked at me as I rolled down the hill.

At the bottom of the hill there was a bar that I saw each time I went to Veronica's house. I had never stopped. That day I stopped. I backed into a space near the door and pulled some quarters from the ashtray. Enough for a beer while I waited for Veronica to come get me.

The bar was dark and smelled like the bartender had pissed in the mop bucket before cleaning the floor. Two men played pool.

"What'll it be?" the bartender asked me.

"Golden's," I said, "in a bottle."

"No," he said, "we only serve good beer here."

The tap was at the other end of the bar.

"What do you have on tap?" I asked.

"Milwaukee's Water."

"Anything else?"

"Nope."

"I'd like a Milwaukee's Water, please," I said.

The beer looked like lemonade and tasted like beer that astronauts would take into space. The bartender never smiled. I would have to come back sometime.

The best thing about drinking cheap beer is that you can drink more for less. After my third beer I called Veronica.

"Where the hell are you? I've been waiting for an hour! The goddamn food is…"

I hung up the phone and went back to the bar. I had

enough left in me for one more beer. Being yelled at made me thirsty. The final beer tasted best of them all. The payphone I had used began to ring. I ignored it.

The bartender answered. He had one crossed eye and I would swear he was watching me with it as he picked up the phone. It was for me. I sipped the beer and took it with.

"You bastard!" It was Veronica. "Don't you hang up on me!"

"You knew where I was."

"Caller ID, asshole. You're down at the Gaslamp. I should have known you'd be at a bar. Are you drunk yet? Are you..."

I hung up the phone. She would be there soon enough. I sat down and finished my beer.

Rap 5

VERONICA NEVER SHOWED and I was out of money. I went home and got high. I pulled a couple of balled-up dollar bills from my coin jar and walked down the street for a sixpack of beer.

The walk was never longer. Every dog barked at me and nipped at my heels. All my neighbors jeered me. A sewer pipe under the street was leaking. A luxury car drove through a large puddle and splashed me good. My fly was stuck open, a big chunk of fabric caught in its teeth. My embarrassment was as exquisite as it was common. I walked on.

The grocery was small, and I saw Manny behind the register. Manny was the owner and always greeted me.

"Hello, Manny," I said.

Manny ignored me. I looked at him. He was stiff and sweating behind the counter.

I turned to go down an aisle for beer. There were two men in ski masks standing in front of me with shotguns. I turned to Manny.

"I'd like a pack of menthols, please," I said.

"Get down on the floor!" one of the men with the guns said.

"Whatever you say, man." I got down on the floor. What would Harvey Keitel do, I thought. I could take them, both of them if I had the opportunity. I was a well oiled machine.

"Do you mind if I have a cigarette?" I asked.

The other man told me to shut up as he looted the register. I recognized his voice. He was this fellow used to live a couple streets away in the same apartments as me two years before. His name was Ted. We had gotten drunk together many times. He was a surfer with no front teeth. I felt nostalgic there on the floor. We had dropped acid once and spent the day at the beach, and now he was going to rob me.

It was then I noticed there were two other people on the ground down the aisle. One of them was Veronica. She was blocking the beer case.

"What are you doing here?" I asked Veronica.

"I've been looking for you," she said.

"Here I am," I said.

Ted told me to shut up again and empty my pockets. I pulled out my cigarettes first. He grabbed them from my hand.

"No," I said, "please, not the cigarettes. Take me instead."

The other man was at the front door now. He told Ted to hurry up. Manny had also recognized Ted's voice. As Ted was leaving with my cigarettes and Manny's money, Manny pulled a large handgun from under the counter. He fired but missed. The plate glass shattered.

"I know who you are you sonofabitch!" Manny yelled. He ran out into the street and fired again. He ran after them, yelling.

I stood up and went to the beer case. Luckily none of them were hurt in the melee. I laid my crumpled bills on the register and received no change. The sixpack, Veronica, and I walked back to my place.

Rap 6

THE NEXT MORNING WAS SUNDAY. I woke up and sat at the typewriter. I sat there for half an hour and stared at the blank page. It was too early in the day to write. I was still too optimistic.

We had fucked for three hours after the robbery. The near-death experience had made me horny. Now I was relaxed. My thoughts were clear. I pulled a cigarette and a ten dollar bill from Veronica's pack. I slipped on my loafers and walked to the liquor store for a pint of gin.

It was a long walk and the store was out of gin. I settled for rum. I didn't feel like walking home. I sat on a bench and sipped the rum. I chased it with a can of grapefruit juice. The bus that ran near my house was coming down the street. I flagged it down.

There was a newspaper on the seat next to where I sat. I picked up the front page. There was a picture of Manny and he looked pissed. The headline read: "Three Men Sought In Downtown Robbery." Three, I thought. I followed the article, which continued on another page.

On the other page was a picture taken from the surveillance camera behind Manny's deli case. It must have been taken right after I walked in. I was standing there and there was an arrow drawn over the photo which pointed to my face. Mine was the only distinguishable face. The picture was clear. I folded the paper neatly and placed it on the seat next to me.

There was one other person on the bus, a blue-haired lady. She stared at me. Her purse was clutched on her lap. The driver kept looking at me in his mirror. While I had been reading we had passed my stop. I hit the rum and finished the juice. The bus slowed to pick up another passenger. When it stopped I got out. I had a longer walk home now. I sat on a bench.

A squad car drove by. I was sure I would be thrown to the ground and arrested. I found a payphone and called Veronica. She was asleep.

"Where are you?" she asked. I told her. "What are you

doing there?"

"I got on the bus, Gus, but rode it too far," I said.

"Why didn't you get off at the house?"

"Please," I said, "just come get me. The cops are after me."

"Why are the cops after you? What did you do, Mudd?"

"I didn't do anything. They think I robbed Manny last night."

"You didn't rob Manny."

"Yes, I know I didn't rob Manny, but the police think I did," I said.

"Are you drunk already? You know how paranoid you get when you drink during the day."

"I'm not drunk. Will you please come get me?"

"I'm not picking you up if you're drunk."

"Alright, you don't have to pick me up," I said. "Just bring me a pack of cigarettes. Then you can go. I'll stay here on this bench for the rest of my life." I hit the rum. "Then you'll be rid of me. You won't have to…"

She hung up on me. I waited for two hours and finished the pint of rum. I had a decent buzz. I decided to walk home. She's not coming, I thought.

Veronica liked to fuck more than drink. I liked to drink, then shag it. I liked to drink after also, especially if the sex was good. That bugged Veronica, the after-drink. She didn't understand. Our differences made us compatible, to a certain extent.

When I got home she was gone. There was a note saying the police had been there. The note also said that she could never love a man who would rob a friend's store. I could never tell when she was kidding. That's what I liked about her. She created a sense of wonder. I pulled a long butt from the ashtray and smoked it. It had ashes on the filter. It tasted alright. I sat down and began to type.

Rap 7

THE POLICE CAME BY AGAIN later that night. I poured us all scotch and sodas. We talked cordially for about an hour. Once in a while we were interrupted by one of their walkie-talkies, but they ignored them and turned the volume down. Eventually they both shut them off and I put on some music. I poured another round of drinks. The lights were turned way down low. They left convinced of my innocence.

Before they left I bummed a smoke from one of them. I went out back to smoke and look at the stars. It was dark and I could hear my neighbor, Nicky, working in his yard next door.

Nicky had won his house playing slots at an Indian casino. During the day he cleaned kennels at the local dog pound. He could barely afford the property taxes. He was a man of high hopes and an indomitable spirit.

I looked over the fence. He had a work light hanging from a tree. He was pressing artificial turf on what appeared to be a flat concrete deck. An edge kept rolling up, and he kept pressing it down.

"It's dark tonight," I said.

"I'm building a putting green," he said. He was hard at it, sweating. "Goddamn it!" he said, pounding the turf.

"Alright," I said. I went back inside. When I was in the kitchen I couldn't remember why I had come in. I got a beer from the fridge and went back outside.

The green was being built on top of a fountain pool that had never held water. I had pissed in the fountain the night he had built it a year before, jinxing it. I looked over the fence.

"You filled in the fountain with concrete," I said. He didn't know I had cursed it with my juice.

"I need to learn how to golf," he said. "There's an opening at the pound for an assistant dog catcher, and I told my boss I could play." The edge rolled up again. "Shit! Shit, shit, shit!"

"Alright," I said. I was drunk and stoned when I had pissed in his fountain. I was drunk now, but wasn't high. I went back inside. I remembered what I had forgotten earlier. I got another beer and went back outside. I handed it to Nicky. We drank. We stood silently admiring his work.

"It's a little small," I said.

"No," he said. "No, no, no!"

We finished our beers in rapid silence. Then he threw his empty bottle at a wall beyond his alley fence. Glass popped and shattered, and lights came on and dogs began barking.

"Well, have a fine evening," I said, turning and going back into the kitchen. When I was safely inside I heard Nicky yell "Fuck you!" at someone across the alley. Nicky was crazier than Veronica and twice as mean. He kept me limber when she wasn't around.

Veronica was the love of my life, the wind beneath my wings. All of the drinking I had done that night made me want to wag it. I called her house. A strange man answered. I hung up and rolled a joint.

Rap 8

ABOUT THAT TIME I BEGAN HANGING AROUND this professional boxer named Jimmy Blake. He was up and coming locally, and I had an idea to write a profile of him. He was a heavyweight with a third grade education. He had lost part of his tongue in a street fight, part of an ear to a meat grinder, and made a career of having his bell rung. He hesitated before finishing his thoughts, so proving an easy target to those who were unaware of his pugnacity. We hung out for a few days, and I was able to sell his story to a local sporting rag. Then I discovered he liked to smoke crank.

Jimmy had an inflated torso and a short temper. I was a drunken stoner whose conversational style attracted antagonism. It was our inability to communicate and our drawing of dissention that bonded us. For a month we were best friends.

He had a solid connection. We smoked speed all night

and all day. The house was never cleaner. Even the oven got a good scrubbing. When I couldn't sleep, I drank. When I drank, Veronica would call.

"You're drunk," she would say.

"Yes," I would say, then hang up the phone. Jimmy would fire up some more crank. My breath smelled like a PCV valve.

Rap 9

WOMEN LOVED JIMMY BECAUSE he was big and stupid. I loved Jimmy because he attracted women. Veronica hadn't called in a month. I thought about giving up drinking. I wanted to give my relationship with Veronica a chance. It would take time. Meanwhile, I would have to be constructive with my sobriety. I had an aunt in Ohio who collected rubber stamps.

Jimmy was on the couch between two groupies, watching a match on television. I told him about my idea of collecting rubber stamps.

"Fuck...off," he said, without looking away from the match.

I got two beers from the fridge, one for him and one for me.

Rap 10

A WEEK LATER VERONICA STILL HADN'T CALLED. Jimmy's connection had been busted. He was jonesing on the couch, watching the tape of a recent championship bout. The contender had bitten off a piece of the champ's nose. They showed it again and again on the replay. Jimmy was shuddering.

"Hey, man," he said, "you got any...beer?"

"No, Jimmy," I replied. "I drank it all."

"Go buy…thum," he suggested.

"Can't," I said. "Just spent my last fiver on a new typewriter ribbon."

He moaned a little as his options began to run out.

"You muth got…thumthin," he said, as he stumbled into the kitchen.

There was a bottle of cheap white wine that I was saving for later. I needed to act fast. He was sure to find it. I heard the fridge opening.

"While you're in there," I mentioned, "pour us each a glass of that wine that's on the bottom shelf."

It was a gallon I had started the night before. I heard its deep, resonant thunder as he popped the already loose cork.

"Aw man, thith thit's…thkunky," he said.

Hesitation, then I heard two glasses tinkling.

"Bring some peanuts too," I said.

The peanuts were too much to ask. I heard breaking glass. I had pushed him too far. I had forgotten how sensitive Jimmy was to authority. He appeared in the hallway, trembling.

"I'll bring you thum wine," he whispered, trying to contain himself, "but thum goddamn…peanuth? Uh-uh, no way. I ain't your goddamn…thlave. Get your own fuckin'… peanuth."

With that, he stormed out the door and into the night.

I went and got the bottle from the kitchen counter. I chose a glass from the cupboard and sat back down in my easy chair, holding the bottle close in case I needed it.

Rap 11

THE NEXT EVENING I SAT DOWN TO WRITE. After Jimmy left I had fallen asleep in my easy chair still wearing my clothes and cradling the bottle. The skunk wine had spilled across my midsection, and soaked into my clothing and the fabric of the chair. I did not change before sitting at the keys, and the pungent odor of dried plonk drifted upwards in search of my nostrils. It found them.

The day, that shit had been hella hot. Santa Ana winds had blown over the mountains into town with their dry and invisible anger. I stared at the keys. They stared back. The odor drifted.

I slipped into my loafers and headed to the market for more wine. Manny's was out of the question, for the time being. The other store was closer anyway.

As I rounded the corner of the school across from the house the setting sun blinded me with a heated sky of bright orange. As my eyes adjusted I saw a man in a wheelchair waiting at the bus stop a block ahead.

It happened so fast. From behind the bus stop shelter suddenly came a woman who swiftly grabbed this man by the hair and began slugging him in the face. I was headed for this. I squinted through the mystical, screaming sunset. Behind me I checked the street in case I had to cross.

It got worse. Before it got worse, which seemed like a long time because she was pounding him pretty good, but before it got worse I thought of Veronica. I shuffled ahead. I began thinking about the wine I was about to buy. Then I smelled my shirt. I wondered about the last time I had washed my hands. I asked myself if I loved my mother.

The beating continued. Others were closer and did nothing except take sides and cheer. I checked behind me on the street again to see if it was clear. Then the tide turned.

After a short exchange of fist and slap the man in the wheelchair managed to grab the woman's hair. He pulled her across his chair, and was swinging her around like a prehistoric street fighter, punching and jabbing at her. I walked straight ahead.

She took the blows well. Finally she escaped his hold and swung her medium-sized, black duffel bag at his head. He ducked like a pro and she walked off.

"You fuckin' psycho fuckin' bitch!" he screamed.

"You fuckin' motherfucker!" she screamed back.

"To you, fucking cunt!" he continued. "Have fun with fucking Steve!"

"Eat my ass," she finished, huffing down the street.

He was still yelling at her, but I blocked it out and

crossed the street. A man in a wheelchair and a woman with a duffel bag, gone. I thought about Veronica. I thought about my mission.

I got two gallons of wine at the store.

Rap 12

THE NEXT MORNING I WAS FLAT ON THE GARAGE FLOOR, reeling with a gutter wine headache. I opened an eye a crack. The light hit it and burned into my brain. I turned away from the light. The blood in my head shifted and produced a stabbing pain somewhere behind my nose. I imagined Jesus driving a railroad spike into my ear with a sledgehammer forged in woe. Ah, my sins. I reached for the wine at the foot of the bed.

When I sat up I began to puke so I ran into the house for the toilet. I didn't realize how dizzy I was. I rammed my face into the doorframe before I made it through to the bowl. I threw, flushed, then threw again. As I was heaving I had an epiphany of poetry. I washed my mouth and checked to see if I had any splashed on my pants. I was clean. I strode to the words.

I sat there for five minutes, but in the distance from the bathroom to the keys I had lost the epiphany completely. Nothing. What becomes of the beautiful revelation? A brief glimpse as the blood fades and crackles like electric dust into the past. A burp rose, and I tasted the previous night's wine.

I still had a fair quantity of weed stashed away for just such an occasion. A spur was needed in the side of that goddamn horse called poetry. I rolled a joint and smoked.

A morning fog had rolled in since the sun had jabbed me in the eye, and now a soft glow masked the optimism of the day. Maybe it was the weed. I gaped at the neighbors next door mowing their grass, but my head still hurt and I didn't feel stoned. I rolled another joint, this one twice as big, a real hooter, and smoked it down. I thought about waxing the antler. I hadn't heard from Veronica in weeks. I returned to the ivory keys of truth.

The thrill was gone. I concentrated on the blank page but it only mocked me, laughing at my literary impotence.

"You stupid fuck," it said, "how dare you attempt to fill me with meaning. You are shit and you will never sell another word as long as you miserably exist." Then it laughed again, "Ha, ha, ha."

My head began to droop. It swung and rocked back and forth for a moment until my chin rested on my chest. A glob of drool rappelled from my bottom lip. I was out.

I woke with a start, fevered and ready. I swatted behind me. No one was there. Only the silence. The ghost. The fear. I had finally devolved into some lunatic caricature of metaphysics. Then the voice spoke.

"More wine," it said, "more wine."

Yes, I thought, that must be the answer.

"No, you fool," the blank page said, "what about me? What of your craft, your love, your life?"

I pushed away from the keys. Then the voice.

"Go, young Prometheus," it said, "grab the fire and make it your own. Take the wine, take it, take it..."

I stood and stumbled backward. I considered the wine, but then I felt the gods of peristalsis lay their hands on me. I returned to the alimentary throne and sat in contemplation, but it was a false alarm. I looked at the tub next to me and decided what I truly needed was a long, hot bath. Then I looked closer, at the grime and mildew growing voraciously across the whiteness of its porcelain. A roach crawled from a crack near my shampoo. I would have to clean it before I could take respite. Only five minutes, I thought.

An hour later the mold had relinquished its hold on my vessel of bodily salvation. I had defeated the knight of sanctimonious decay and would now celebrate in the sweaty broth of inspiration. I made for the door to disrobe. Before I got two steps I slipped on a puddle of water that had formed on the linoleum. I reached for the sink but it was too late. I was down again, back flat and toes up. They would find me this time and shoot me for sure, like a poor broken horse not fit for glue.

I had been down for five minutes when the phone rang.

It was Veronica. I could hear her voice on the machine in the other room. I reached for the shower curtain to help me up, but I pulled it down, ring by ring, like in that movie. The call ended and I heard a click.

A helicopter circled overhead, thumpa thumpa thumpa. My head was limp and began to spin. The smell of stale urine wafted around me from the base of the commode. Almost honey. Not cleaned in two years. The back of my head was wet. Rubber stamps, I thought. Sadness and bilge water, rats and the crowns of kings.

Then I remembered. Six month previous, during a bender at the house, I had half finished a bottle of Puerto Rican rum, and staggered into the john where I had wisely hidden it from the madding crowd. Unless someone had found it in the interim it would still be there. I leaned up from my repose and cracked the cabinet. There it was, shining silver, grand and alone, a lighthouse or ransom. I reached, unscrewed, drank and fell back.

"This writing will be the death of me," I thought as I lay on the floor. I had been forced to go into writing by my need to support the drinking and drugs, the good life. Now it was one or the other, the work or the muse. Prone there on the bathroom floor I chose the other. So be it.

Rap 13

"YOU SHOULD STOP DRINKING," Veronica told me once.

"I am too self-righteous when I'm sober," I replied. "I drink to level the playing field."

That was a while ago.

Jack had gone to his parents' house up north for the weekend and taken Tipsy with him. I was alone for two days. I put on a good pair of white pants and went down to the Horseneck Café to level the playing field.

The Café was crowded. I found a stool at the bar and drank beer. Two men were playing pool, and when they finished one of the men sat next to me and ordered a hamburger. As he waited for his burger he fidgeted with the napkin under his drink, slowly peeling the edges away, then rolling the pieces into tiny balls and placing them in a row on the bar. When he finished off his napkin he did the same to the label on his bottle.

I saw all this through the corner of my eye, but pretended not to notice. Soon the label was gone, pressed into service alongside the napkin. I raised my bottle to order another and level the playing field even more.

"Hey," he said, leaning his face over my arm, "you weren't usin' that napkin, were ya?"

I handed him my soggy beer napkin. He made quick work of it. My cold beer arrived. I could tell he wanted to say something more.

"I lost my business," he said.

"You did," I said. "It's alright."

"Vermiculture," he said, sidestepping my shallow absolution.

"Vermiculture," I repeated in acknowledgement.

"You know, worms," he said. "I was a worm farmer."

"Check, please," I said, motioning to the barkeep.

While I waited he began telling me everything there is to know about raising and selling worms. His voice hissed like an overflowing toilet and smelled just as bad. I had a decent buzz going, and worms were the last thing I wanted to hear about. I stared straight ahead at my reflection in the mirror. I needed a shave.

He must have become insulted by my lack of attentiveness because he took off his glasses and began poking me with them. I looked at him. His beady eyes were glowing and fluctuating as he described the loss of his beloved worms. He had a tremendous overbite and when he spoke he looked like a dog chewing on a glob of peanut butter.

Finally his hamburger arrived. I got up to go, and ran right into my robber friend, Ted, the man who had rolled me for my cigarettes at Manny's.

"Hey," he said, "sorry about that one night."

"No worries," I said. "Let me buy you a beer."

"It's on me," he offered.

We sat down.

"What did you pull?" I asked.

"Not enough to justify the effort. That bastard Manny almost killed me."

Our beers arrived. We toasted each other. It was a good time. Then all hell broke loose.

As I tipped my beer to drink the worm farmer grabbed my wrist.

"The worms have arrived," he whispered. "They're here."

Then he stood up and announced it to the whole bar.

"The worms are here! They're in my burger, the worms are in my burger!"

Everyone stopped what they were doing. The jukebox song ended just then, and the room was silent. The worm man let go of my wrist and grabbed his burger with both hands. He held it above his head and began squeezing it so that the meat crawled out from the bun. Looked like worms to me.

"Is this some kind of a joke?" Ted asked.

"Check, please," I said, but the bartender was concerned with the worm man.

There was ground beef and onions all over the bar now.

"Only ketchup will kill them!" he screamed. He reached down the bar for the nearest bottle of ketchup. He spilled drinks, but no one moved. They were silent, mesmerized. When he had the bottle he began anointing everyone within ten feet with ketchup. It was a mess. He was out of control.

"I'll save you all!" He turned to save those behind him, but slipped on a greasy hunk of beef and went down hard. Our savior had knocked himself out.

When the room regained its senses Ted dragged his body out the door by his feet.

"Cut his balls off!" someone yelled.

I finished my beer and walked out. I met Ted at the door as he was coming back in.

"You've been hit," he said.

I looked down. My nice white pants were covered in ketchup.

"Cigarette for a dying man?" I asked.

He obliged. I left him with a pat on the back.

I was out of smokes so I turned down the alley to go to the only store open. Ted had dumped the worm man's body in a pile of trash next to the building. I almost tripped over his legs as they jutted out. I left him there to slumber among the worms.

Rap 14

THERE MUST HAVE BEEN A FULL MOON THAT NIGHT, I can't remember. To enhance the cigarettes I chose a bottle of rotgut at the late-night store. As I was lifting a three dollar gallon from the bottom shelf an old woman in a nappy sweatsuit noticed my ketchup-stained trousers.

"Jesus and the devil," she cried, "somebody call an ambulance!"

I reached out to calm her, but she dropped her bread and backed up.

"Don't you touch me," she said.

I walked toward her and the register. The cigarettes were there. A little girl came around the corner. She saw me and began howling. Her mother came to see what the ruckus was and began screaming too. It was an evil dance of circumstance.

"It's ketchup," I said, but the mother and the daughter continued to scream and ran out the door.

"Don't you hurt them," the old woman warned, making some ethereal motions with her knotty hands. She was still backing out the door when she bared her teeth at me in an intimidating display. I set the wine on the counter.

"Menthols, please," I said.

The cashier recognized me. She found nothing unusual in the fact that I would walk around covered in ketchup or blood. She sold me the smokes and I found my way home.

Jack was home early with Tipsy.

"Are you okay?" Jack asked.

"It's ketchup," I said.

Maybe I was bleeding. I couldn't tell. I sat down with a glass of wine. The playing field was now level.

Rap 15

THE NEXT MORNING CRIED RAIN. All night my dreams had been filled with nomadic worms attempting to repatriate themselves with their master and guardian. The rain on the garage roof lulled me in and out of sleep. There would be worms on the sidewalk today. I smelled coffee. I stretched a sweater over my head and went into the kitchen.

From around the corner in the living room I heard a strange but familiar music. Bass guitar and saxophone. I filled my mug and followed the piper.

The living room shades were drawn. Jack was on the couch with his legs up. Tipsy was on the floor watching television. There were two dogs on the screen. They were humping, really going at it. A pug and a Boston terrier. The pug was giving it to the terrier. They were locked doggystyle, uttering various whimpers and moans. The pug turned and flashed a wicked grin at the camera, then began growling and grunting.

"Dog porn," I said, sipping my coffee.

"It's for him," Jack replied, passing the buck.

Tipsy turned to me. His eyes were crazed and dilated, like he wasn't there.

The action on the screen was heating up. Both dogs were now howling in junkyard ecstasy. Tipsy twisted suddenly and threw his head between his legs, licking himself. The pug and terrier climaxed together. Tipsy followed suit.

The music cut abruptly from sax to a smooth, nylon string guitar solo. The scenario also changed. Now the pug was meeting a Chihuahua over a bowl of kibble. They sniffed each other's ass and the pug mounted. I picked up the video boxes.

"*Hot Dogs*," I read, "and *The Bitch Is Back*."

"This is *The Bitch Is Back*," Jack said. "The terrier is the Bitch."

I sat down to watch. The rhythm of the music was slow and churning. The Bitch came back and did that horny pug good. By the end of *Hot Dogs* Tipsy was flaccid. Jack had fallen asleep. I warmed my coffee, and went back and watched *Bitch* again.

By the end of my second viewing I had finished the pack of smokes from the night before. My hands were warm so I ran them under some cold water. I thought about Veronica. We hadn't spoken in over a month. The rain relaxed my heart. I stole a pack from Jack's carton in his room and dialed her number.

"So, are you drunk?" she asked.

"No, but my hands are kind of warm," I said.

"What does that mean, Mudd?" she asked. "You are so drunk, you're confusing me."

The phone was cordless, so I cradled it between my ear and shoulder while I unwrapped the pack. I put the cigarette to my lips.

"Hello?" she said.

I lit the cigarette, and blew out the smoke cool in front of my face. I meant to say "You should come over," but I began coughing violently. Jack smoked filterless clove cigarettes, and I had misinhaled thinking I was getting less. I couldn't breathe. I began stumbling and kicked the leg of the coffee table. The large glass ashtray flew off and hit Tipsy square in his nuts. He woke with an almost human shriek. He began barking and running around the room in circles, dragging his ass on the hardwood floor.

"Hell-lo?" Veronica said again. "What the fuck is going on over there, Mudd? Are those jailbait bitches there again?"

I could barely keep the phone against my ear. My toe felt like it was broken for sure.

"She's a...Boston...terrier," I muttered through clenched teeth.

"I should've known," she said.

Tipsy was still screaming. Jack was awake now, yelling at Tipsy. His voice added to the confusion. Things were happening quickly. I heard Veronica say something about the East Coast and wolf pussy. Then she hung up.

"Hello?" I said.

I hung up and Tipsy limped back across the room. He was still in one piece. I had almost looted his family jewels and now he wanted to be friends. I picked up the ashtray. He came over and licked my hand. I loved Tipsy. He loved me.

The clove burned low in my mouth. The smoke stung my eyes and blinded me. The phone began to ring, but I had placed it on the coffee table. My eyes were closed and watering. I pinched the cigarette from my lips and thought I was ashing it in the tray, but the red hot cherry found Tipsy's muzzle instead. The dog let loose another belligerent howl. I stabbed my hand blindly in the direction of the ringing phone. I found it. It was Veronica.

"It's me," she said. "Sorry about the 'wolf pussy' comment. That was really counter-productive of me."

"Alright," I said. "I almost spayed Tipsy."

"You don't spay boy dogs," she said, "you neuter them. I knew it, you're wasted."

My eyesight was returning. At my feet I saw Tipsy crouching silently, nursing a toothy glare. His eyes were locked on mine.

"You should..." I started to say, but Tipsy leapt for my throat. He had me on my back immediately. I could smell the singed hair on his snout.

"I should what?" Veronica asked.

"You should..." I wheezed.

"What, Mudd?" I could hear her voice lose its patience. "Sounds like you're ready to pass out already. Call me when you're sober, asshole."

Then I heard the click.

I didn't deserve this much love. Tipsy must have heard Veronica hang up because he loosened his death grip from my throat. He sat back sidesaddle on his haunches to protect his cracked chestnuts. His tongue dangled and I thought he was smiling. I sat up. My neck was wet and smelled like dog breath.

Tipsy had almost killed or maimed me on numerous occasions, but he always knew exactly what he wanted and how to act to get it. My friend, Tipsy Russell.

He picked up *Hot Dogs* and brought it over to me. I was

redeemed. I brewed a fresh pot of coffee. We would be friends forever. We sat on the couch and I rubbed his belly and he licked my hand and we watched *Hot Dogs* three times that day before it was due back. He even fetched Jack's carton of clove cigarettes from his room for me. I would buy Jack another. All was right and it rained the entire day.

Rap 16

THE RAIN EVENTUALLY STOPPED and the worms crawled out onto the sidewalk to die in the sun. It was a Saturday morning. The rain had jumpstarted my creativity. I was able to bang out a couple of obscene poems and a dirty short story. I walked in the warm morning sun to the post office to mail them to my favorite editors.

My neighbors no longer shrank away at the sight of me. Their smiles were benevolent, wistful even. Nicky was in his front yard chipping golf balls into a bucket. He had a Miniature Pinscher tied to the fence behind him. There was a spiked collar around the dog's neck. The dog began snarling and baring his teeth at me as I approached.

"It is morning, and Nicky is the sun," I said.

Nicky was in the middle of his stroke. He missed the bucket, but drove the ball into the side of his house.

"Fuck!" he said, slamming his wedge into the ground. His grass was filled with divots. The Pinscher continued snarling. Nicky looked up at me. He only had one long eyebrow that stretched over his eyes, and it was furrowed and clenched.

"You didn't come to my party," he said.

"I didn't know you had one," I said.

It was nine in the morning and Nicky was finishing a beer. He rifled through a cooler at his feet and pulled out two cold ones. He popped one, sipped, then threw the other to the now silent but grimacing dog. The dog bit into the can, and beer froth shot everywhere, drenching the tiny beast's head. That little dog sucked his can dry, like he was sucking milk from the teat. Nicky set up another ball.

"Your game's coming along," I said, as he began his backstroke. He stopped and glared at the ground. He picked up his beer and drank.

"That's why I had the party," he said, setting up again. "I got promoted to assistant dog catcher. My boss said I sucked so bad on the golf course it made him look good."

The dog had finished his beer. He was growling and pulling at the cord that held him fast. His eyes were black with the tar of hate. He wanted my blood.

"Anyone puke?" I asked, as Nicky began his down stroke. This one he popped in the air, over the house. A divot the size of a small pizza landed close to the bucket. Nicky stared at the ground. His eyes began bugging.

"Just Tiger," he said, dragging on his beer. "Some dumb shit gave him whiskey."

"Tiger was there," I said, nodding. "He seems well behaved on television."

"The dog," Nicky insisted, jabbing at the Miniature Pinscher with his wedge. Tiger was drooling and snapping. I could hear the clacking of his teeth.

"Shut up!" Nicky said. He tossed another beer to the obviously thirsty dog. Again, the same method of consumption.

I had never seen the dog before. I lit a smoke. I had one left I was saving for the walk to the post office. I offered it to Nicky.

"Your friend likes beer," I said.

"Brought him home from the pound. We bonded."

"A little dog named after a big cat," I said.

We finished our smokes and I took off without saying goodbye. To the end of the block I could hear Tiger's aggression. Then the sound of breaking glass and Nicky yelling "Fuck, fuck, fuck!" It all seemed to mean something, but I couldn't figure out what it was.

Rap 17

I MARCHED TO THE POST OFFICE. Saturday morning meant yard sales. Veronica liked yard sales. We would go once a month. Sometimes I was able to buy a beer or a hooter from the friendly ones. It made their wares more lucrative for the buying.

That Saturday I was alone and my pockets were empty of spare change. I needed to mail the manuscripts in my hand. Living in a friend's garage was cheap but not free.

The St. Ignatius church down the block always had some tables out. Most Saturdays I passed them without hesitation. That day I stopped for a brief look-see.

"Make me an offer," the young man said.

He shot out his hand like a Vegas barker.

"I don't see anything I need," I said.

He ignored me.

"Anything," he continued, "make me an offer, let's talk. Let's make a deal."

There was a bronze, middle-aged man reclined in a lawn chair behind him. He was well dressed with neatly trimmed salt-and-pepper hair, and wore enough gold to pay my rent for a year. He was the pit boss, clergy disguised as a golf pro. I would have to introduce him to Nicky. He seemed to be guiding the young man with magical passes of his hand.

"I'm only looking now," I said.

The boss did his hand trick.

"How about these?" the young man said, producing a pair of running shoes. "Hundred bucks in the store. I can let you have 'em for..." he spun his head to the boss. The boss silently nodded his head. "...twenty-five bucks. Twenty-five and they're yours."

I did need a new pair of shoes. Seventy-five percent off was quite a deal.

"I don't have any money on me right now," I said.

"Twenty dollars," the bright young man said. He whipped his head around. The boss gently closed his eyes and nodded again, this time more subtle than a king.

"Twenty dollars," the young man repeated as he

produced a cloth and began polishing the already spotless shoes. "I'll throw in the laces for free."

The boss's guiding hand began slowly tapping like a pendulum on the arm of his chair. I could barely hear his rings rap as they made contact. I was being drawn in.

"Really," I said, "I don't have any cash…"

"We take credit," the young man said, producing a veteran validating machine.

I felt the boss's hardening stare. He wanted me. He wanted this sale. I stumbled backward, making promises.

"Will you be here all day? I'll stop by later. I have to get to the post office now, before it closes. I'll see you later."

I was walking backwards up the sidewalk when I said this. I turned and hurried my pace. As I turned I heard the pit boss speak.

"Call the cops if he doesn't come back."

I quickened my pace. The hair on my neck bristled. I looked straight ahead.

In the next block both sides of a duplex had their stuff on the lawn. There was a large group milling about. When I saw them all I intended to pass them up. Instead, something caught my eye.

It was a wooden, Oceanic mojo idol, about a foot tall. Mojos were Veronica's passion. I could make it a gift for her, a peace offering. I only had one ten dollar bill in my pocket. I had planned on paying for the manuscripts' postage and stopping for cigarettes on the way home. Surely the change from the postage would be enough to cover the yard sale trinket. I would forgo my daily ration of cigarettes for love. The sale's tenders were casually monitoring everything from the front porch. No pressure. I waded into the crowd.

As I lifted the mojo to check the price I was rapped sharply on my left shin by something hard. I almost folded right there.

"Put it down," a voice hissed. "I saw it first."

My eyes began to water from the pain. I set the mojo down and turned to meet my aggressor.

She was small and quick, darting in front of me like a flyweight. She was clearly more than ninety years old. Her chin had sunk away, and her nose projected like a draftsman's tool. These two features recalled a grotesque human badger reflected in a wavy circus mirror. The top half of her face was concealed behind large, opaque shop glasses which prevented me from guessing what her next move would be. She put her hand on the mojo.

Neither of us saw the other woman. She materialized from the crowd and latched onto the mojo along with the badger. There was a tense moment of silence.

"Back off, Phyllis," the second woman said.

Phyllis didn't budge.

"You lose, Gladys," Phyllis said. "Take your hands off the statue and step back slowly."

"I need this one, Phyl. Don't do this to me," Gladys said.

"Make your move."

Gladys made her move.

She grabbed the mojo but Phyllis' grip remained firm. Gladys began kicking at her ankles, trying to take her out from down below. Phyllis was resilient. It was the myth of King Solomon. They tripped on a table leg and went down, wrestling in the grass. The mojo broke free and rolled to the ground at my feet. It didn't matter to them anymore. They had tasted each other's blood. Now it was personal.

A crowd had gathered around them. A man began taking bets. Phyllis was getting three-to-one. I picked up the mojo. Its carved lips smiled tenderly up at me. I circumnavigated the crowd and paid. It was less than I had expected, a bargain.

"Earl, break that shit up," the matron of the sale told a burly man seated next to her.

As I walked down the street with the mojo, Earl waded into the crowd. Two doors further a roar erupted from the scene. A winner had been declared.

Rap 18

I COULD SEE THE BLUE MAILBOXES of the post office up ahead a block. Mojo was tucked securely under my arm. The sun glowed with proud hope in his blue morning sky. I knew then that there would be a tomorrow.

A house three driveways from the post office had a yard sale almost every weekend. I sometimes browsed but it was mostly junk. Today I passed without a glance or a nod. Again, something snagged the attention in the corner of my eye, a drop of dew on a leaf of grass, a sparkle of gold among rough wooden odds and dull brass ends.

I stopped. I focused. My heart raced with discovery.

It twinkled like a mirage. I blinked and rubbed my eyes. There, amidst the leftovers and throwaways, the knicks and the knacks, sat a 1950 Olivetti Lettera, the Holy Grail of manual typewriters. Brushed aluminum hull, adjustable spring-loaded keys, weighing no more than a pound. Rumored to be extinct outside of private collections. I began trembling.

This yard sale lacked a bounty of contending shoppers. I surged with confidence. The only others were a gargantuan man-child wearing a triple-oversize football jersey and dark, pumpkin-like sunglasses, and his diminutive, flea-like mother. They were nowhere near the Lettera. The Giant was pumping up and down on his tiptoes, waving his hands in the air, and calling out incomprehensible syllables and groans, while his mother darted among the tables of gewgaws twenty feet away.

There it was. The closer I got, the more real it became. I forgot the manuscripts. I forgot Mojo. I forgot myself. I kneeled in front of the find, the prize. A Lettera would have been impossible to duplicate, it was so pure in its perfection. I set Mojo and the manuscripts down, and reached a hesitant finger out to touch it. Yes, it was authentic. I would pay any price.

A blank page was in its spool. My fingers shook like a novice archaeologist as I typed my name. It was as easy as thinking it, the machine uttering barely more than a whisper of a rap. It was truth.

Then a shadow fell over me. It was the Giant. He was moving unrepentantly on me, quick for his size. He covered the ground between us without grace, rubbing his belly with one hand and the back of his head with the other. I lunged backwards to save myself, only to see his sledgehammer foot come down in a statement on the Lettera, completely crushing its rare and delicate frame.

"First down!" he hollered, picking up a football and throwing it against the side of the house.

"Julius, put that down!" his squirrel of a mother ordered, following him like an aberrant wake.

"Two-thirty, left! Hike!" Julius the Giant hollered again, lifting a worthless glass jar and hurling it to the ground. He was a mad tornado, a behemoth of lunatic energy.

"Julius, I said to put that down," his mother repeated, "so put that down, we're leaving."

She reached up and grabbed his belt to pull him backwards. I ducked under a sturdy desk. Then I saw Mojo and my pile of manuscripts where I had set them on a table. I could only watch.

Even in reverse Julius the Giant's mammoth hands were grabbing. They barely missed Mojo, but somehow found the entire stack of sealed manuscripts. He tore them in half, then quarters, then eighths, then stuffed as much as he could fit into his mouth and began eating them.

"Hut-hut-mmmnrrw," he mumbled, his voice mired in the mastication of shredded paper and envelope.

"Save your appetite, you fat turkey," his mother said.

He spit out the manuscripts and began moaning insensibly again as she dragged him down the sidewalk.

I emerged from under the desk. I felt as though I had just experienced rough sex. The Lettera was destroyed. I picked up Mojo.

"The King is dead," I told him.

A man in a bathrobe with a cup of coffee came out the door of the house. He looked at the trail of wet pieces of paper. He followed it back to the smattering of demolished gimcracks until his eyes rested on the remains of the Lettera. The man's mug shattered when it hit the ground. Julius the Giant's work was complete.

"Long live the King," I said, stashing Mojo under my arm and heading back to the house.

I stopped at the store on the way. With no manuscripts to mail I could afford cigarettes. Tomorrow, as well as love, was saved.

Rap 19

I HAD BEEN LIVING IN JACK'S GARAGE for three months longer than I had planned. Eight months total and still no million dollar advance. The spring was hot. There was only one small window in the garage, and a crack around the door. It smelled of gas and oil and tools. There would be no more rain until October. Nothing moved in the garage, not even the flies.

My money had run out. I would have to begin panhandling or find a legitimate job. My stories hadn't sold. My poems weren't selling. No one was interested in my letters. My well had dried up. That million dollar check was a pipe dream.

I had twenty dollars to my name. I sat in the garage, too poor to sweat. Then I heard it. Dying men hear angels singing, or harps, or their mother's voice. Mine was a whimsical, electronic tinkling. It moved closer, crawling up the street. I lifted my head. Yes, it was true. 'Pop Goes The Weasel.' In this neighborhood that meant one thing...Miguel, the ice cream man. I grabbed my twenty and headed out the door.

Miguel was parked at the far end of a few blocks. He rolled in a tricked-out ice cream truck, but sold more than ice cream. He had connections across the border, and smuggled in regular shipments of homemade tequila, Cuban cigars, and Puerto Nuevo lobsters. He was an entrepreneur. Children of all ages looked forward to seeing Miguel. My mouth began to water as I hurried up the street.

I walked fast, my hands in my pockets, each clutching a ten dollar bill, singing a Freddy Fender song, 'Wasted Days and Wasted Nights.' I shuffled so fast my chankla got caught on a knob of concrete sticking up. I went down hard on the side of my face and kissed the sidewalk. I stood up. My face was raw.

As I brushed myself off I saw an old man on the porch of the Evening Wood Nursing Home, rocking back and forth in a chair. He was watching, eyes scoping me from under a shock of white hair. He must have seen me just bite the dust, but he didn't show it. No concern, no laughter, not even acknowledgement. I could hear his chair creak, just rocking back and forth, a face of stone.

I moved on. Miguel was kicked back in the driver's seat, heels on the dash, smoking a cigar.

"Hola, amigo," he said. "I have not seen you for some time."

"Buenos fundidos, Miguel."

"What can I breeng for you today, my friend?" he asked.

"I have twenty dollars left. After this I am nothing," I said. "Set me up with a feast."

Miguel must have been a brother in a past life. He disappeared into the rear of his truck and rummaged around for a few minutes. He reappeared with a brown grocer's sack stuffed full.

"And for you, my friend," he said, a sudden twinkle of magic in his eye, "een honor of your poverty, I would like for you to have thees."

He lifted a key from around his neck, unlocked a secret compartment in the floorboard, and produced an unlabeled bottle sealed with a cork and candle wax.

"Thees, my friend, ees my last bottle of El Pulque, La Leche del Diablo," he said, putting it in my sack.

"I've never heard of pulque," I said.

"Eet ees the finest dreenk een all Mexico, so pure eet ees ageenst the law," he assured me. "My friends, they make eet themselves."

I imagined a fine Kentucky moonshine I had tasted years before, sealed with tin foil and a rubber band, and kept in a mason jar in the back of a friend's refrigerator for only the most special occasions. It had tasted like spring water and was as clear and cool as your conscience when you drank it. This pulque, this gift of purity and spirit might be just what I needed. Miguel was right on.

"Gracias, Miguel," I said, handing him the two tens.

"No problem, my friend. Thank *you*," he said, stuffing the cigar back in his mouth, and sitting back to wait for his next customer.

I walked home with the stuffed sack. It may not have been a million dollars, but at least it was worth another night. The old man in the rocking chair on the Evening Wood porch watched me as I hurried past. He was a scarecrow, a dead plaster cast.

I was staring at him as I tripped on the same concrete as before. I nearly spilled my sack, including the mysteriously divine pulque, but I recovered. I sang Freddy Fender to myself. Thanks to Miguel the night would not go to waste.

Rap 20

VERONICA WAS ON THE COUCH WHEN I WALKED IN THE DOOR.

"Surprise, baby," she said.

It had been quite a few months since we had spoken. We were erratic, but picked right up again where we left off. She ashed her smoke, and hugged me and the sack.

"You went shopping," she said, peering into the bag.

"Tonight we feast," I said, "so that tomorrow we may die."

"You're a poet," she said.

"I'm a bum who writes. I've even got a Longfellow."

"But you're a cute bum," she said, following me into the kitchen. "I couldn't wait to see you again."

She loved me like a drug. We were made for each other. I barked like a dog. I set the sack down. She saw the side of my face that was marred.

"Oh baby, what happened to your face?"

She went into mommy mode. I cracked a bottle of tequila and took a long drag, then dabbed some on the bruised side of my face. She kissed my bruise, then licked the rest of the tequila off.

"Mmmm, that tastes good. What's for dinner?" she asked, rubbing her body up and down the side of my leg.

Miguel had hooked us up. Besides the tequila there were at least five pounds of fresh lobster meat and sea bass, eight Cuban cigars, a small bottle of bootlegged mescal, two peyote buttons, el pulque, and two ice cream sandwiches. I pulled lemons from the fridge, salt from the cupboard, and we did shots for an hour. Jack was home. He sported some beer and we cooked up most of the lobster and sea bass. We spent the next four hours eating and drinking. Around sundown we each spent another hour savoring a cigar.

"I have something for you," I said to Veronica on the back porch. I went and got Mojo.

"Baby, he's beautiful," she said, stroking and fingering his wooden crown.

"I had to fight for him," I said. I accentuated my words by doing a shot of the mescal.

"You're such a man," she said, drawing me close. Her hair smelled of apples, fresh as the Garden of Paradise. "Let's go lay down on your bed."

We were buzzed. I had saved the best for last. Jack had gone to the store for more beer. The sky was turning lavender. A cool evening breeze made its way across our faces. Now was the time.

I went and got the pulque and some clean glasses from the kitchen. I sat back down outside and cracked the wax seal. Without hesitation I pulled the cork cleanly from the bottle with my teeth. I was the last man on earth. I was Hemingway, I was Malcolm Lowry, I was Pancho Villa. I poured us each a glass.

"What is this?" Veronica asked, as if she were expecting some sort of exotic aphrodisiac, a kinky, wry smile cornering her lips.

"It's called pulque," I said. "Miguel says it's like a Mexican moonshine, a sort of alcoholic delicacy."

The pulque was milky, with a frothy consistency. Veronica held it to her nose for a whiff.

"It smells like shit," she said, her face drawn back tight.

I smelled mine. Shit indeed.

"What's it made out of?"

"I don't know," I said.

Veronica feared very little in the world. She tipped the glass, finished half, then tilted back the rest.

"Tastes like shit too," she said from a grimace.

I drank mine down. Shit indeed.

"Gimmee another," she said.

I heard Jack's truck pull up out front. He came out back

and handed each of us a beer.

"Have a snort of pulque," I said.

"Pulque?" he huffed. "Fuck that shit. Is that what you're drinking?" He smelled the bottle.

"It just smells bad," I assured him.

Veronica was downing her third glass.

"What's wrong with it?" she asked, wiping her chin.

"Nothing's wrong with it," Jack said, "if you don't mind drinking Mexican spit."

"Spit?" she said. Her eyes glazed. "What the fuck are you talking about?"

She was drunk and I could tell by her tone that she was, in some way, about to become obstinate.

"Old men sit around chewing on agave cactus, then spit into gourds with holes in the top. The saliva helps it ferment."

Veronica was overcome with seriousness, and her expression clouded a pale green. Jack popped the top from his beer, took a long draught, and continued.

"Then they take the gourds and pour the stuff into huge wooden barrels that have been cured on the inside with pig shit."

"Sh-sh-sh-shit?" she stammered. "And sp-sp-spit?"

If Veronica had been blown with clear glass I could have seen the entire evening rise from her stomach like lava before she projectile vomited all over poor sober Mojo. Then she puked on the ground, and made her way to the bathroom in the house, tossing lobster and pulque and tequila and beer all the way. Tipsy had fallen asleep from all the leftovers. He woke up and began lapping the spew from the ground, following the trail into the house.

"That's what I heard," Jack said. "I also heard the Aztecs used it as a hallucinogenic. You may be seeing purple flames and flying dinosaurs in a minute."

I could hear Veronica retching in the bathroom. Then the water faucet. I cracked open a cold beer, sipped, then poured another glass of pulque.

"Flying dinosaurs, huh?"

"Yep."

We toasted Miguel and the purple flames. Venus was

rising in the east, shining blue and green against an indigo sky. I toasted her as well, for she would be the only love I would be getting that night.

Rap 21

THE DINOSAURS NEVER SHOWED, and Venus was in the sky on the other side of the planet. Veronica was hungover as a dirty nun. I wasn't much better. She moaned through clenched teeth that she needed me to drive her home. She had sweated profusely all night, and the smell of her perfume now singed the single pillow. It hung like a bad dream in front of my nose. Combined with the garage smells of gasoline and tools and a pool of vomit one of us had left in the darkness it created a brew that sent me staggering to the washing machine. I dry heaved for a couple of rounds, then my stomach managed to lob up a glob of hardened bile the size of a peanut. Much better. I hit the wash button, delicate cycle.

I stuffed her bra and shoes into a plastic bag. She groaned like a mental patient as I hoisted her over my shoulder and carried her to her car. The early morning fog was thick, and the rooftops still glowed a bright, humming green, illuminated by the light of the pulque. I shook my head and the glow vanished.

Veronica's car was more reliable than mine, but it had no suspension and it exhausted a black cloud that invaded the interior when it was started. I put the car in gear and lowered the windows. She always kept an extra pack of smokes in the glove box, which I raided to freshen up a bit.

During the night Veronica had rolled over in her sleep and started scrubbing my zucchini. Just before I climaxed she passed out again. I had intended to finish the job myself, but before I could formulate a quick fantasy I, too, passed out. Now my balls sagged like leavened dough that refuses to rise. The pressure had built, and was crawling into my stomach and numbing my legs. Driving would soon be out of the question. I would have to take matters into my own hands.

I undid my pants and began washing the fleshy cucumber. At first there was the pain, but as I drove on it slowly melted to pleasure. I had never pulled the pink carrot stick while I was driving, and aside from the lack of shock absorption the vibration and hum of the engine felt kind of good. It wouldn't take long.

My eyes rolled up into my skull. I imagined I was driving my fleshy cucumber instead of Veronica's car. My fingers were now the accelerator rather than my foot. There was no brake. This was a vehicle that wanted to crash.

I rolled through a stop sign, and my venous veggie stick changed to a jet controlled by a supersonic joystick riding between my legs. I became an eagle soaring across the endless skyway. My god was drawing near. Then I heard a voice.

"Where's my shoes?" Veronica asked, raising her head slowly. "What are you doing?"

"We're almost there," I said.

"Are you playing with yourself?"

"The car could use some shocks," I said.

"Here, let me help you with that."

She slid across the seat and pulled my hand away from its duty. The cucumber was now an eggplant, gorged and thumping with expectant ecstasy. She took it into her mouth and bobbed up and down a few licks. Her lips were slobbering wet and full of love. The feeling was exquisite, worth all the damnation life had to offer. Then she stopped. I looked down. Her eyes were closed, and she was snoring with my squash-hard, average-sized penis still in her mouth.

The pressure returned. We hit a massive bump. Her head hit the bottom of the steering wheel. Her eyes flickered open and she let out a weak "awwwmmn" before she passed out again. We hit another bump, and her teeth gripped the cucumber ever so slightly. One more jolt like that and I would be a stub, barely a beety root vegetable. With a shaky hand I braced her head from any further turbulence.

Veronica lived in a small bungalow on the edge of a canyon. As I pulled her from the passenger seat a pack of coyotes laughed in the foggy canyon below, and the freeway buzzed unseen in the early morning distance. I braced her like a corpsman. My balls aching and my gut wrenching we staggered across the threshold.

"Hey, Veronica, it's about goddamned time!" a foulmouthed voice said. "Why don't you come over here and blow me?"

Veronica kept a bird, a half-blind and verbally abusive Hyacinth Macaw named Cosmo. He thought he was her pimp because he was all blue and yellow, and was very protective of her. If he saw her straying to me or the drink he would attack, but he could never tell who was in the room.

"Veronica's not here," I said, dragging Veronica across the room.

"Veronica's here, Veronica's here, blow jobs for everyone, awwrrakk!" Cosmo screamed.

I flopped Veronica down on her bed in the back room.

"Veronica's not here!" I yelled down the hall.

"Step right up, folks, best blow jobs in town. Drop your socks and grab your cocks for Veronica!"

Cosmo began singing the Elvis Costello song, drawing it out, singing in sha-la-la-las, taunting every nuance in those four syllables.

I undid Veronica's clothes and pulled the covers over her. She revived.

"Unngh, I had a dream," she moaned, "that I was waxing your toy soldier."

She was adorable, even while stinking, but my balls were dangling like participles. I wanted to gain portage, but she was unconscious again. I had to do something soon or my legs would go numb.

"Veronica, get in here and make your daddy some fish fucking tacos!" Cosmo was unrelenting, even for a pimp.

Veronica had told me once that she would be upset if I didn't take advantage of her, even when she was passed out, as long as she had intended to be taken advantage of in the first place.

"Veronica's not here," I said, unbuckling my belt.

As I leaned over to kiss her, my crotch nestled against the corner of the bed where her comforter had risen into a soft, flesh-like mound. Before I could get my pants off the deed was done. I shuddered and my hips instinctively began humping the bed. Hours and hours of love and pressure unloaded into my pants. My spine electrified and I buried my face in the comforter.

"Hey, Veronica, bring me a goddamn cerveza!" Cosmo screamed from the other room. "Today!"

I would be worthless for the rest of the day. I stumbled into the bathroom to wipe the excess glue from the inside of my trousers. I checked my face in the mirror...broke, humbled and unshaven. I hallucinated, and the bags under my eyes became alligator skin covered with stickers that said things like "Niagara Falls" and "Timbuktu." Through the tiny frosted window I heard the neighbors' alarm clock go buzzing in a mechanical, static rhythm, flat-lining them awake. My knees buckled.

I dragged my weakened body to the front room.

"Hey, Veronica, give us a little head, buddy," Cosmo whined as I sat on the edge of the couch.

"Who?" I said.

A door opened and Veronica's neophyte roommate, Cindy Bunks, post-doctoral genius of Catalonian protest music, came down the hall. She was wearing only a long sleeping shirt and blonde pigtails. She looked at the spot on my pants.

"Tracks. Nice. You are so common," she said to me. "You know this, right?"

Cindy turned around and walked back down the hall.

"Veronica's not here," she said, slamming the door behind her.

With my testosterone gone my head began to pulse with each beat of my heart. I rummaged through the three ashtrays on the coffee table and found an inch-long roach that seemed to hold some salvation. I fired it up.

"Hey, Veronica, you tramp, give us a puff!" Cosmo ordered.

His eyes never left mine. I walked over to him.

"Veronica's not here," I said.

I took a long, thoughtful drag, then blew the smoke in Cosmo's face, Cosmo the blue-feathered pimp, Cosmo my friend. A minute passed. The room was silent, then...

"Hey, Veronica..." Cosmo began.

"Veronica's not..." he began again.

"Veronica's not...awwrraak..." His voice trailed off. He began rocking back and forth on his perch, easily and silently marching nowhere, to what appeared to be a reggae beat.

"Veronica's not here," I said, reeling heavily from the consequences of my actions.

Cosmo ignored me and began ripping into his birdseed. Even pimps get the munchies.

I ambled two blocks to the bus stop, and fished the miracle change needed for a fare from my pocket. I waited. The morning had become an obscured, dull burlesque. Its fog would remain for weeks, the sun hiding like a god, as elusive as caviar.

A southbound alley scavenger pulled up on a squeaky beach cruiser hauling a trailer of aluminum cans. He expertly felt through the barrel next to my bench. I recognized him. Oftentimes I would see him in the alley behind Jack's house.

"South is a good direction," I said.

He gave a low, incomprehensible growl, and continued chucking cans into his trailer.

"I'm just gonna hop in," I said, nodding to his trailer.

"Uhh-uhhhhh-urgh," he explained, stopping his work only briefly to lift one gristled eyebrow at me.

I lowered myself into the carriage, gently immersing myself in the soon to be recycled cans. He threw a few more cans on top of me, then mounted his steed and we rattled away.

The cans were warm, and if I didn't shift myself too much the sharp, thorny edges of aluminum didn't pierce my side. The familiar odor of tangy, stale beer mixed with the ever syrupy cola flavors. This odd sentimentality, combined with the possibility of lacerating pain, insulated me from the chilling fog. The scavenger was in no hurry, and the gentle swaying of our forward motion soon had me snoring like a baby, not aware his bough was ready to break.

Rap 22

TIME PASSED. I hadn't heard from Veronica in quite a while. The months of fog still blanketed us like a moldy omelet, neither chicken nor egg.

Nicky was over at Jack's for happy hour. Jack had cleaned out his den to rent, and the new tenant, Francois, was slouching in the far corner of the couch, holding a can of Milwaukee's Water on his chest. I was reading the want ads. We were watching a golf channel.

"Hey, Francis," Nicky said, "I hear in France if you want to get drunk you just ask somebody on the street and they'll give you the money for a bottle of wine."

Francois turned to me.

"Why does he zay 'Francis'?"

I lit a cigarette.

"My name es Francois." He turned to Nicky. "My name es Francois."

"Is it true, Fran-sees?"

"Only eef you are France," Francois said. "I am Quebecois, North Americain."

"What the fuck does that mean?"

"Not eef you are Americain. Not for you," Francois said, wagging his finger.

Nicky ignored him.

"Does he spik English?" Francois asked me. He sipped his beer.

I circled an ad. I had been out searching for work all morning. The past couple of weeks I had earned some cash as a temp cleaning office buildings. They let me go when they discovered me smoking a joint with another temp in a stockroom. Now I ran through the roll call of menial labor for an unemployed writer. Laborer, landscaper, retail, driver, dishwasher...

Nicky went to the kitchen and came back with a handful of cold, uncooked smoked sausages from the fridge.

"Eat it like you stole it," I said.

Francois was surfing channels.

"Hey, Frankie, turn it back to golf," Nicky said through a

mouthful of sausage.

"Ze golf et es nozing. I em to sleep."

"Gimmee that fuckin' thing," Nicky said, grabbing the remote. "Didn't your parents teach you anything?" He turned it back to golf and opened a beer.

"My fathair he es magistrate, retire-ed, from Montreal. My pair-ents, zey move to America."

"You came here with your parents? You're almost forty years old!" Nicky huffed. "Why the hell don't you live with them?"

"My fathair he does not spik et me. He says to my fami-lee I em drug addicted."

Francois pulled a thumb-sized pipe from his pocket. He cleaned the lint from the bowl. From his other pocket he pulled a small glob of hashish wrapped in a piece of scratch paper. He rolled a tiny, oily ball and dropped it in the pipe.

...warehouse, telemarketer, installer, grocery, auto detailer...

Francois hit the pipe three times, then put it back in his pocket.

"What the fuck, Francis Prince Albert Sinatra!" Nicky said, leaning forward. "You gonna bogart it all, you French fuck?"

"My name es Francois, and I em not ze France. I tell you I em from Quebec, but you do not leesten. You do not smoke-ed me when you have ze smoke."

He pinched another nugget from his wad and passed the pipe to me. I took a drag and passed it back to Francois. He passed it to Nicky.

"Scraps, huh Kermit?" Nicky said.

Francois' eyes were beginning to sink into his skull.

"Why does he zay 'Kairmeet'?" Francois asked, melting into the couch. "I geeve him what he ask-ed for."

...customer service, data entry, taxi driver, sales, bartender...bartender...

I circled 'bartender', folded the paper under my arm and said "I gotta go."

Rap 23

THE AD SAID "APPLY IN PERSON." I walked very slowly to my car. The hash was kicking in. I was parked a few blocks away, and by the time I got to my car I had forgotten what it looked like. I tried my key in the door of one that looked a lot like mine. It worked.

I knew where the place was that I wanted to go. I knew how I wanted to get there. The car was running. The radio was on. My confidence was high, but somewhere between the time I started the engine and the moment I decided to leave almost two hours had passed. I blinked. I would include 'patience' as one of the virtues on my application.

I put the car in gear. Instead of rolling the car shuddered and went nowhere. I stepped on the accelerator and turned the wheel. Still no dice. The car rocked again, and I realized the flashing lights I had seen from the corner of my eye for the last five minutes were not a product of the hashish. I looked in my mirror.

A tow truck had backed to within inches of my rear bumper. I looked to the side of the truck. The driver stood there with a ponytail and a greasy smile. His hand was on the control panel. He spit a vicious stream of mouth tobacco on the ground, and my rear end lifted in the air.

"You're towing my car," I said, stumbling out.

"Registration's expired," the driver said, squirting another tobacco stream to within inches of my shoes. "It's bein' impounded."

I hadn't renewed the plates in three years. I explained to him that I forgot and would do it first thing tomorrow.

"Too late," he said, smiling and removing his gloves as he jumped in his truck. "It's considered an abandoned vehicle, a derelict. You've got no choice."

He laughed in my face. His final spitter hit my pants just below the knee and dribbled down. I quickly retrieved my bottle opener, some discs, and a lighter from my back seat, then watched my car disappear backwards down the street and into the fog.

I stood there with my salvaged items and watched his

mildew-colored spittle drip slowly onto my foot. This was a sign to take the rest of the evening off.

A streetlight flashed on above me, amber in the lowering fog. In its waxing light I noticed a white-haired figure, a man rocking easily in a chair on the front porch of the Evening Wood Nursing Home. As the light burned to full strength it revealed nothing in his expression. He was void of dialogue, an urban Rushmore. He was only a face.

Rap 24

WHEN I GOT BACK TO THE HOUSE Nicky and Francois were drunk.

"Did you get jobs, Mudds?" Francois asked.

He stood to light a cigarette. He was bent like a question mark, and swayed trying to match the flame to the end of the cigarette. He lit it and sat back down.

"My car got impounded," I explained.

"Oui, like my car," Francois said, "but I was drunk-ed."

There was a documentary on the television showing some kind of war.

"Hey, Francis, you green goblin, why don't you give yourself up and get me a beer?" Nicky said.

Francois sulked deeper into the cushions. He pouted his lips and stared straight ahead at the screen. Following a moment of silence he turned to me.

"My name es Francois."

"I'll add ten minutes to your life if you give me a cigarette," I told him.

Francois stood again. He dressed like a physics professor, pleated slacks and button-up short sleeve shirt, but instead of a pocket protector he kept his cigarettes there. He was a cigarettes professor. He pulled one from its box and handed it to me. I leaned in and he lit it for me, nearly melting the tip of my nose.

"That hot girl came by while you were gone," Nicky said.

"Veronique," Francois added.

I ashed my smoke. Tipsy wandered in, looking bored. He noticed Francois' outstretched leg. He sniffed his pants, then mounted and began violently humping Francois' leg.

"Ha, Tipsy likes frog legs! Get 'em, Tips, give him the red rocket," Nicky said.

Francois turned to me.

"Why does ze dog he do zis?"

I went to the fridge and got three beers. By the time I returned Francois had a stain on his leg similar to mine, different color. I handed a beer to Nicky. He opened it with his teeth. I opened another and handed it to Francois.

"Merci, Mudds."

Merci indeed.

Rap 25

I FOUND WORK IN A WAREHOUSE ACROSS TOWN. We moved boxes around all day. Every day. The place was cavernous, and smelled like apathy with sweat.

The receiving clerk was a tall man with skin the color of dust and cardboard. He wore a dirty blonde rug on his head. Every time he would sweat the wig would shift slightly, and a green pus would ooze from underneath. Dale, the forklift driver, told me the clerk used to be a meth chef, and had set his head on fire when his lab exploded. His hair had never grown back. Dale sold him weed for his pain.

In front of the whole morning crew they would play games of warehouse chicken. Tom, the receiving clerk, would walk under the prongs of the forklift just before they were lowered. He would taunt Dale with his hands, daring him to drop the forks on either side of him.

"C'mon, Dale, you pussy," he would challenge. "I've already died once. What can you do to me?"

Tom would beat his chest like a caveman, then they would laugh about it. When Tom was out of earshot Dale would add:

"Fuck you, Tom. Fuckin' jerk."

Eight o'clock every morning we wandered in, sipped some free coffee in the break room, then loaded the trucks for their deliveries. We warehoused and delivered office furniture. First thing in the morning Tom would come to me. He would take me to a five-hundred pound desk.

"Pick that up," he said, pointing to the desk with his hand full of invoices.

He always had some bills of lading or packing slips or invoices in his hand. I lifted the desk onto a moving dolly. Tom looked around.

"No," he said, "put that down."

I lowered the desk back down. His hands twitched in a nervous tic, slapping the inside of his wrist against his belt when he was thinking or about to get upset. I waited and anticipated as he stood there spanking his belt, looking up and down the aisle.

"Come with me, young Mudd," he decided, leading me to the darkest, hottest corner of the warehouse. He slapped his belt all the way there.

"There's four hundred of them," he said, nodding at three rows of stacked and boxed office chairs, "and they all need to be opened."

It was hot and a line of green ooze was creeping down his temple.

"I love the smell of cardboard in the morning," he said. "It smells like...hey, where's my box cutter?" He walked away, wiping his brow.

Each box had a fine layer of dust coating it. The dust scattered into my face each time I broke down a box. I sneezed for an hour and my eyes watered. Just before the morning break Dale drove up.

"Tom got you doin' this, huh? What a dick," he said.

"I saw the ooze," I said.

"Yea, what the fuck is that? Glue?"

I pulled a chair from a box and sneezed.

"Don'tcha hate that?" Dale asked. "I always go home with big, black boogers from this place. Aw, fuck it, let's go to break."

Rap 26

DALE GAVE ME A RIDE HOME. Before we left the parking lot he packed us a bowl.

"Try some of this shit," he said, pulling onto the street.

He cranked his radio, classic rock. I bent down in front of the dashboard and smoked.

"If I could shit pot I'd smoke my own turds," he said, taking the pipe from me. He steered with his knees, and didn't bother to bend down.

I pulled a sticky, brown wad of snot from my nose, rolled it, and threw it out the window. He passed the pipe back to me.

"So have you met Jerry yet?" he asked.

"I don't think so," I said, passing the pipe back.

"Is it cashed?"

"I think so."

He pulled open the ashtray and pinched some more off a small bud. He packed it and smoked it.

"You'd remember Jerry," he said. He hit the pipe again and passed it to me. "You got your chauffeurs license yet so you can go out on deliveries?"

"No, not yet," I said, taking a big puff. I tapped the bowl empty out the window and handed it back.

He opened his cigarette box, pulled out two, and replaced them with the still hot pipe. We smoked the cigarettes.

"So do you do anything creative?" he asked.

"I write," I said, "but the bottom fell out of my market. Now I move boxes around."

"I hear ya. I play drums in this heavy metal band, and people come to see us, but..."

We drove the rest of the way in stoned silence.

Rap 27

"THIS IS THE PLACE," I said. "The beer's cold inside."

"I stopped drinking when I got married," Dale said. "I started collecting rubber stamps."

I got out of the car.

"I need a nickel," I said.

He opened the ashtray and handed me the small bud. I handed him a five, but he refused.

"Don't worry about it," he said, turning up the radio. He smiled a crooked-tooth smile, flashed a goats head sign with his hand, and thrashed back and forth as he drove away.

Rap 28

I GOT UP BEFORE THE SUN THE NEXT MORNING. In the low light of the garage I packed and swatted a bowl. I made some coffee, and stood on the front porch toasting the surfboard in the pre-dawn darkness.

The bus was filled with quiet souls. Every so often a hand would reach up and pull the cord that rang the clunky bell telling the driver to stop. I sat in the rear over the engine where it was warm. The coffee had gotten me on the bus, but the wake-and-bake was putting me back to sleep. My head nodded once and I fell asleep.

In a minute I was dreaming, at my desk and rapping the keys. A butler leans over me and pours me a glass of cabernet.

"Will that be all, Sir?" he asks.

"Yes," I say, waving him off while still typing. "Take the rest of the day off."

"Thank you, Sir," he says.

I can hear him packing his day bags in the kitchen. I am at my desk in the garage. The glass of wine has disappeared. I hear the front door close. I am alone.

Then I am on the bus again. The driver gets up while the

bus is rolling down the freeway and offers me a glass of wine. I hold my empty glass out into the aisle and he pours me full. The bus rattles and he apologizes for spilling part of my drink. Then he goes back to the driver's seat. I am not alone. I have the glass of wine.

I was kicked awake by a combat boot to the shin.

"Do I know you?" a rough voice asked.

I lifted one eyelid and cut a glance. I thought I was still dreaming. She was popeyed and had a livid scar down her left cheek that Georgia O'Keefe would have appreciated.

"Are you a friend of Weird Bob?" she continued. She leaned in close to examine me with her good eye.

"No," I said, "I don't know Weird Bob."

"Whistlin' Joe?"

"From Kokomo? No, I don't know Joe."

She backed away and pulled a cigarette from behind her ear.

"Ever done any bodyguard work?" she asked.

I could smell last night's whiskey and this morning's tobacco on her breath. I looked at my arms. Grapevines. They could barely type.

"No bodyguard work."

She thumbed a lighter and lit the smoke.

"No smoking on the bus," the driver said.

"Yeah, right, sorry, forgot." She pressed the flaming cherry into her palm. A strange, green smoke rose and drifted between our heads. She put the half-burned stick back behind her ear. The popeye turned on me again like a spyglass.

"Wait...you just started at the warehouse."

"Bingo," I said.

"Here," she said, handing me a paper coffee cup. "Freshen your breath."

I took a modest hit and began gagging, mostly from glee. The cup had some coffee in it, but held a majority of some single malt beverage, scotch most likely. I caught my breath and handed the cup back.

"Thank you," I rasped, clearing my throat.

"Too much coffee, huh?" She pulled a flask from her bag and drew some more scotch into the cup. The bus driver was scoping us in the rearview mirror. She took a drag and handed the cup to me.

My dreams had come true. I was awake. My breath was fresh. I pulled the flaccid cord and the bus groaned to a halt at our stop.

Rap 29

HER NAME WAS CARMEN. Her hair was cut in a reverse mullet, shaved bald on the bottom, and she walked like a professional linebacker. She had everything but a postmodern face, meteor crater complexion and a raised eyebrow above the popeye. The morning sun rising in the east warmed our backs as I followed her into the warehouse.

Everyone hailed her as a potentate when she walked in. Tom walked by with his invoices, and she punched him in the gut while she threw her other arm around his shoulder.

"Hey, Tommy!"

Dale was climbing onto the forklift. She slapped him on the ass. Then she began shadow boxing with three guys at once, growling and spitting at their feet. She was poetry. The warehouse was her page. It was a grand entrance.

"Come with me, young Mudd," Tom said.

He took me down the aisle to the same five-hundred pound desk as the day before.

"Pick that up," he said, slapping his belt.

I bent and lifted. Halfway up my feet slipped and I bit the desk hard with my teeth. My head rang and my vision dimmed. I felt sick and belched out a ruddy, moist cloud of coffee and scotch.

"Don't let that desk kick your ass," Tom said.

I opened my eyes and got another grip.

"Move it right here," he said. He was five feet away.

The wheels on the moving dolly squealed with age as I pushed it.

"Okay, set it down. I'll be right back."

As I leaned it down my cigarettes fell out of my pocket. It

was a sign. I lit one and waited for further instructions. Cardboard dust shadows cut through the air, riding on sunrays that shone in. It was morning. I thought of all the yard sales I could afford now that I was employed. I thought of Veronica. I would call her on lunch.

"There's no smoking in here, Sir."

Tom had snuck up behind me.

"Come with me," he said.

He led me to a five-drawer, lateral fire file. Walls of concrete surrounded by plastic and steel. Titanium locks. Average weight, one-thousand pounds.

Tom looked at the moving dolly in my hand, then in my eyes. He sucked his lips back to his teeth, then into a smile as he nodded his head up and down. I began nodding mine. I knew. He started laughing as he turned and walked away, reading his invoices. At about twenty paces he threw his head back and roared with amusement. I was alone with the monolith.

The file was in the loading area. Everyone was moving furniture onto trucks for delivery that day. I set the dolly down. My eyes were still crossed from the blow to my teeth. I checked to be sure they were all still there. My alphabet was intact. No soup tonight.

All I had to do was lift the file up, roll the dolly under and set it down. I got a grip. I lifted. Beads of sweat danced on my forehead. I envisioned ogreish, mammalian Soviet Bloc power lifters covered in chalk on Saturday afternoon television. I reached blindly for the dolly with my foot. The forklift drove by and honked.

"Jerry's on his way out," Dale said.

My hands were cramped and my palms were sweating. I couldn't see if the dolly was where I wanted it. I let the file down slowly. Onto my toes. There was a sound not unlike the crumbs at the bottom of a bag of tortilla chips being crumpled to be thrown away. I was pinned. The file was silent.

I smelled smoke. Jerry walked behind me. He was smoking a cigarette. He was talking rapidly and pointing at things with the two fingers that held the cigarette.

"Okay fellas, we gotta hurry up," he said, "but take your

time. We don't need any crushed toes."

I was bent and hugging the file now, kissing the Blarney, the holy Kaaba, trying to get it up again. My ears were shot through with the adrenaline of survival. I was deafened to any noise coming from my mouth, even though my lips were moving. As my hearing faded in and out I realized that I was mumbling and murmuring in some extinct, prehistoric language. Jerry stopped talking.

"Hey, who's praying?" he asked, twisting his head like a confused man who hears a mosquito but can't see it.

I let loose with what I figured would be my final grunt on this earth, but in a flash the file was lifted. Pain shot up my legs, along my spine to my head. I reeled backwards and bumped into Jerry, smashing the back of my head into his cigarette. Someone told me later it looked like an arc welding class. I smelled burning hair. Jerry propped me up and continued talking.

"Let's get a move on, fellas," he said, clapping his hands. "Take it easy out there today."

Carmen was lifting the fire file like it was a fortune cookie. She had it on the dolly and into the truck in less time than it took me to think about it. She came out of the truck slapping her bare biceps. Someone across the room yelled:

"Check out those guns!"

Carmen posed and stretched. Men whistled and hollered.

I felt the hair on the back of my head. It was crispy. I had put Jerry's smoke out. He moved over to Carmen and pulled two more cigarettes out. He handed one to her and lit it. Then he squeezed her bicep, smiling proud. Jerry had a simple, round face that looked as if it was accustomed to watching cars rust from a back porch.

As they stood smoking Carmen pointed at me. They both watched me rubbing the back of my head. They talked and smoked some more, then Carmen leaned in and caressed Jerry's package. He giggled like a schoolgirl. Her eyebrow raised and the popeye looked dead at him. He hesitated, then they both broke out in wild laughter, puffing away. It was a sign. I relit the cigarette I had started earlier.

"Final warning, Mr. Mudd."

Tom was right behind me. I could hear him slapping his

wrist to his belt.

"No smoking."

"You may have just saved my life," I said. I dropped it and stepped on it.

"Looks like you're going out with Carmen today. Here's your paperwork." He handed me a stack of papers, sniffing the air. "Who's your hairdresser?" He walked away laughing.

Carmen got behind the wheel. We bolted from the loading dock. I didn't know it was possible to burn rubber in a fully loaded, twenty-six foot diesel box truck, but she managed to do it. In each of the first three gears. She saw me feeling my teeth again.

"If you stay at this job you'll be dead within a week," she said, sipping on her coffee and scotch.

"Typing hurts more," I said.

As soon as we hit the freeway she rolled down her window and handed me a fatty.

"Smoke this," she said. "This is ten times better than what you'll get from Dale."

She was right. I don't remember our first three stops. I smoked my whole pack of cigarettes before lunch. We stopped and bought more, plus a pint of scotch and a two liter of soda for the afternoon. Perhaps I would survive after all.

Rap 30

CARMEN WAS AN ARTIST. She was part of an exhibition that Friday at a local gallery. She invited me and put my name on the guest list. I called Veronica. No one answered. I turned to Francois. He was sunk into the couch, kissing his pipe while lighting the ball of hash in the bowl.

"I'm going to go to an artists' reception," I said. "You come too, Frost."

"My name..." he began. He held in the smoke. His eyes closed to a peer and his brow furrowed in thought. He blew the smoke. "...es Francois."

His hand slowly found a bottle of Bordeaux. He poured a half glass and sipped, staring ahead. I waited. He looked at the pipe in his lap, cradled between his thumb and index finger.

"No, Mudds," he said, tilting his head, contemplating the pipe. "Tonight I em here." His head began swimming around his neck.

"Free drinks till midnight," I said.

His head stopped. He squinted at me.

"What times do we leave?"

We left twenty minutes later. The bus driver turned off the lights when he pulled away from the curb. We anted up with the rest of the Bordeaux in the dark.

"Een Montreal one year I study ze art," Francois said, sipping the wine. "Zen I become waiter, sommelier. But zey say I em no good. Zey say I know my job too well." He sipped and handed the bottle to me. He hiccupped, squeaking and bouncing in his seat.

"You were ahead of your time," I said.

The bus rolled and hissed to our stop. The gallery was still three blocks away. Francois pulled the pipe from his pocket, and we finished the bowl we had started while waiting for the bus.

The gallery had a small front, and there were people huddled together outside smoking cigarettes. Inside was dark, and elaborate dance music was coming from some back room. I gave the lady at the front door my name. She looked at me long before checking the list.

"This is my translator," I said, introducing Francois.

"Merci du twat," he said.

She looked confused, as if we were an old joke she never understood.

"He's from Paris," I said.

Her face brightened considerably and she patted me on the chest.

"Why didn't you say so?" she scolded playfully. She handed us each a pass. "Enjoy the reception."

We found the bar. With red wines in hand we moved off to the side to survey the room. Some were dressed in tuxedoes, some wore t-shirts and jeans. Everyone was wearing black. There was a woman making swimming motions with her hands as she described her work. There was someone dressed in a gorilla costume walking around holding the hand of a midget. The gorilla was sipping a bloody Mary, and the midget was eating a banana. A man in a nearby tuxedo was wearing a birdcage over his head. He saw me eyeing him. He broke off his conversation and approached us.

"I hear the weather this year is warm in Paraguay," he said, leaning in.

"I haven't heard that," I said.

"Yes, very warm indeed." He spoke with the flair of an opera impresario. "And you know how the alpacas dislike the heat. It simply sours their coat." He opened the door of the birdcage and sipped his martini, then closed the door.

Suddenly the gorilla began to freak out, jumping up and down and flailing his arms. His bloody Mary went in the face of a woman behind him, and the heel of his foot found the crotch of an aged gentleman to his right. He was grunting and baring his teeth, and let loose a sarcastic primal scream just as the midget pulled out a riding crop and began lashing him. The ape began cowering, and the midget would bait him with the banana, then whip him more when he reached mournfully out for the sweet, yellow prize. In no time the ape was subdued and the midget had strung a leash on him. Everyone in the room applauded. The gorilla and the midget took a bow and moved on.

"Eet es ze birth of man," Francois said. "He has discovered how to control his animal insteenct."

I saw his hand fumbling with the pipe in his pocket.

The man in the birdcage finished applauding. "Bravo, lads, well done. Say," he said, turning to us again, "have you tried Isabella's cakes?"

"Cakes?" Francois repeated, perking up, eyes growing wide.

"They are very delicious," he added.

"Cakes?" Francois said again, growing insistent.

"Yes, my good man, just over there."

The man in the birdcage made a dramatic gesture with

his arm. Unblinking, Francois wandered off in the direction of the man's arm.

"As I was saying," the man in the birdcage said, "the coat of the alpaca..."

He was interrupted from behind. Carmen had snuck in and goosed him with a credit card swipe. He was taken aback and began to fluster, but when he saw who it was his face opened in a cherubic smile.

"Why, Carmen, how good it is to see you," he said, draping his arm around her.

"I see you've met Count Burbot," she said to me.

I introduced myself and shook the Count's hand. The Count turned back to Carmen.

"I was just telling your friend about the warm season they are having in Paraguay."

"Bet the alpacas are hatin' that shit," she said. She had a beer in her hand, and the good eye was dimmer than usual.

The Count didn't miss a beat.

"That's exactly what I was saying to Mister Mudd," the Count said, opening his door and sipping his martini.

Francois returned with a large plate piled high with cakes. His lips and nearby face were covered in the unwiped frosting of greed. He munched greedily, one after the other, downing every other bite with a swig of wine. I ate two of his proffered cakes and was lustily satisfied. He finally cleaned his mouth, and we all followed Carmen into the next room to view her paintings.

On the way Francois filled his plate once more with cakes. He also came back with an entire bottle of wine, which was tucked under the same arm that held the plate of cakes. He poured us each a glass.

"Aren't Isabella's cakes wonderful?" the Count whispered in my ear.

I ate three more.

Carmen was showing a total of five paintings. We contemplated the largest for a moment in silence, Carmen with crossed arms, me sipping wine, Francois eating cake, and Count Burbot opening and closing the door of his birdcage to suck the olives out of his drink. The painting was of a familiar shape. I couldn't quite place what it was. In the middle of the design was a print from the bottom of her boot where she had kicked the canvas with red paint. Francois wiped his mouth and took some wine.

"You see ze lines how zey like Picasso?" he pointed out.

The lines did resemble Picasso. Yes.

"My dear, what do you call this piece?" the Count asked.

"It's called 'Vagina Dentata F.U.'" She sucked dry her longneck bottle.

"I believe this is your masterpiece," the Count added. "Tell me, how do you get the boot print to look so authentic?"

Carmen took a step back, then reared up as if to kick the painting, but stopped just inches short of the canvas. Her legs looked as though they hadn't felt a razor in years, and curly leg hairs flew every which way when she snapped her foot back at the end of the kick. The artistic process of creation had never been explained more clearly.

"Marvelous! Splendid!" the Count said. "I must own this painting."

"Five grand," Carmen said.

"I will give you six thousand dollars, my dear."

"Sold."

Carmen went for another beer. Francois poured us more wine. The Count wrote a check. Across the room on a small stage a man in a beret was rising to speak. The crowd became silent. The music stopped. Everyone awaited his words with breathless anticipation. I felt as if we were all on the threshold of collective transcendence. His mouth opened.

"Gas!" he yelled.

The crowd roared in approval, screaming and whistling above the applause. He stalked the stage while the noise subsided, pacing a figure-eight like a caged beast. The onlookers grew silent once again, filling the prerequisite for his words. He stopped pacing and raised his hands.

"Gas!" he yelled again.

The crowd roared louder this time. Some of the faithful fell to the floor and had to be carried away. People were ecstatic. There was a brief scuffle near the stage, two young women fighting to grab a piece of the performer. He was not deterred. Still he paced. The crowd settled down. A look of anguish came over his face.

"Corn!" he yelled this time.

I didn't think it was possible but the reaction to this was greater than the first two. Tears flowed down adult faces. A woman screamed at nobody. Children were raised high and carried to the foot of the stage as offerings. I sipped my wine and watched it all.

"He es lost," Francois said. "Et ees cry for help."

"Gas!" he yelled again.

The gorilla was going apeshit, and he threw the midget's banana peel at the man on stage. The Count opened the door of his cage and dabbed his eyes with his scarf.

"Gas!"

"Zee world es large," Francois said, "he ees small." He sipped his wine. "He es alone."

"Gas!"

It was an extraordinary scene. It reverberated with clarity and mania. I heard a woman behind me claim it was pure beauty, the essence of love. And then, as abruptly as it had begun, it was over.

"Good night, gasbags!" he yelled before being hustled out of a back door by three large men wearing sunglasses and earpieces. We could hear more commotion outside as he passed, wailing and the sound of shattering glass. It was a few moments before order could be restored to the room. Carmen had sidled up during his exit, sipping on a fresh beer and hooting as he left the building.

"At the end of the night," she said, "we're all going to trash the place, rip everything off the walls, piss on it, throw garbage everywhere, then take a single match and burn the whole fucking place down as a final act of our collective artistic vision."

Francois and I turned to look at her. She draughted her beer and looked at us.

"I'm only kidding," she said. "Jesus Christ."

"Of course you are," I said.

It was then that Isabella's cakes began to work their magic. The midget and gorilla were shaking down the crowd for donations. People were dropping bills and gold jewelry into an overturned top hat carried by the midget. He would bow each time someone dropped an item of value into the hat. As I watched them move our direction I felt my insides begin to roil and gurgle. I burped but it did no good. The closer the midget got, the lower my intestinal distress moved. The cakes were wasting no time.

The midget held the hat in front of Francois. Francois fished around his pockets, withdrawing the pipe and a considerable amount of lint as he turned them inside out. The wine bottle under his arm slipped loose and nearly crashed to the floor. The midget exhaled with perturbed impatience, and drummed his fingers on the bottom of the hat. Likewise, my bowels were becoming liquid with a less than discrete sense of urgency. As Francois searched his person for a donation a great and terrible odor filled the vicinity. The gorilla was the first to begin sniffing the air.

Francois found a quarter in his shirt pocket, and feebly dribbled it in the hat. The midget looked at the quarter in the hat, then up to Francois in disbelief.

"Cheap bastard," the gorilla muttered.

Francois pouted his lips in shame and insolvency. The midget moved to me for a pledge but it was too late. The smell overcame him and his eyes glossed. His face turned gray, and before he could stop himself he was puking into the top hat. I felt a brief protest near the bottom gates of my colon, but knew the defenses could not hold. The last thing I saw before turning to find a toilet was the midget on his hands and knees belching and spitting his bile into the hat of donation and charity.

I located the bathroom without delay. The pot was cool as the cakes came rushing out. I heard the door open, and a man say "Holy fuck!" and leave as easily as he had decided to come in. I waited. I wondered. I meditated.

My side of the stall door had a mirror on it. It was signed at the bottom with a price tag. Art was everywhere. I watched myself. My hair was a mess. Someone had dropped a comb on the floor. I picked it up, looked in the mirror again. I lifted the comb to my head. I hesitated.

"You are a work of art," I told myself. I lowered the comb. My bowels still bubbled. Only a few minutes more.

I had learned a trick once that if you wrap toilet paper around a comb you have a musical instrument. The paper in the stall was anything but supple, but it stayed nicely as I folded it over the comb. I began to play. I ran through a few bars of various familiar songs, Stephen Foster, Cole Porter, then became patriotic. As my anal cavity shuddered and groaned I broke fully into 'God Bless America.'

As I was honking on the comb the restroom door opened. A man came in and washed his hands. The cakes flowed again. They were following the song. I was the Pied Piper of Palaveres. I played harder. The man dried his hands, then held a business card under the stall door.

"Say, Babe," he said, "are you signed with anyone?"

I stopped playing and took the card. Vice President of a major record label.

"No, I'm not," I said, passing the card back.

"Look man, you sound fabulous. What other songs do you know?"

I started into 'Battle Hymn Of The Republic.' He clapped his hands to the beat.

"Whoa, Babe, you knock me out!" He began pulling at the stall door. "Come on outta there." I wasn't moving. "Play another one," he said.

'Dixie' was next. I saw his foot tapping the tile floor. The comb rattled with music. The walls echoed with art. The man was on his knees now, looking under. I paused and looked at him.

"Don't stop, man," he said, wriggling his way into the stall with me. When he was in he stood up and snapped his fingers. "I've never heard anything like it. I've gotta record you." 'America The Beautiful' was next. "Oh man, this is so hot!" He danced in place in front of me. His suit had a wet stain on the back from when he slid under. He was sweating. The toilet paper got soggy so I replaced it and continued. Then the finale, 'The Star Spangled Banner.'

"Out of fucking sight!" he said, popping the latch on the stall door. "Gotta make sure I'm not dreaming." He opened the stall door, then swung open the restroom door. "Everybody, check this out!" he yelled.

In seconds men and women were crowded around the

stall watching me play the National Anthem on the gallery throne. People were singing along. It was better than a baseball game. The song climaxed and everyone went crazy. The man in the suit screamed "More!" and people were yelling "Encore!"

I set the comb down and wiped with what was left of the toilet paper. The crowd watched every move I made. I flushed and they applauded.

"Alright, everyone out!" the man in the suit hollered. When the room was clear he turned to me and pulled out a checkbook from his breast pocket. He wrote me a check for five-hundred-thousand dollars as my first advance plus a signing bonus.

"We're gonna make you famous," he said, shaking my hand. I pocketed the comb and the check. He took off and disappeared into the crowd.

Carmen was elated when I told her. "You are on the road to success," she said.

The Count gave me his card. "If you'd ever like to invest in wool let me know."

I asked Francois to bring us a bottle of champagne. He peered at me with sudden suspicion.

"Why do you needs me to bring you ze wine?" he spat. "Have et yourself, Monsieur Rock Star." Then he wiped his chin in my direction and kissed the air before he staggered off to find more cakes.

The reception emptied out after midnight. I called a cab and went out to smoke a cigarette. I rubbed the comb in my pocket. It was warm folded in the check. Francois was passed out on the curb with one arm dragged in the gutter. The other arm still cradled a bottle of wine, and cake was smeared across his face and in his hair. People stepped over him. When the cab arrived I had to convince the driver to allow me to bring him along. I showed him my check and he laughed in my face.

"Fuck your money," he said. "I need cash to haul that piece of shit."

We finally decided to put Francois in the trunk. When we got home I dragged him across the lawn in the dark. He had puked on himself in the trunk so I let him sleep out on the grass by the surfboard.

I tucked the comb under my pillow and fell asleep. I was George M. Cohan, Yankee doodle-do-or-die.

It was Saturday, the weekend. Of life.

Rap 31

TWO MONTHS LATER IT WAS WEDNESDAY, the day before Thanksgiving. I quit my job at the warehouse as soon as the advance check had cleared. I had practiced my musical art every day for ten or twelve hours a day. My picture began appearing on the covers of magazines. I was scheduled to go into the recording studio within the next week.

The comb had become as famous as I had. It was an iconic instrument, like Lucille to B.B. King. It had STIFFY written on it, and slept in its own jar of blue disinfectant every night. I took it everywhere, always ready for a song.

I was doing ads for my favorite brand of toilet paper. I was booked on late night talk shows. I bought cases of wine instead of bottles. I was negotiating to buy from Jack the house we lived in and turn it into a medical marijuana dispensary. I opened the day's paper: "Local Man Has Much To Be Thankful For." Underneath the headline was a picture of me holding STIFFY. My fly was open in the picture. I folded the paper and placed it on the couch.

The record label had given me four cel phones and a large utility vehicle that resembled a shiny athletic shoe. There was a steel rack welded to the front to shove smaller vehicles and paparazzi off to the side. I had a video screen installed in the visor so I could watch myself while I was driving. There was another so a passenger in the front seat could watch me, and more screens in the rear for people in the back. The marketing team had a large monitor wired to the outside above the rear bumper for the benefit of public viewing.

Francois had stopped speaking to me. He had respected my poverty, but I outbid him for his room, offering Jack double what he was paying. This moved Francois to the garage with the washing machine, where he would smoke hash and listen to Yves Montand tapes until three in the morning. He threatened to sue me. He called his father's attorney to his side. Jack overheard them when he was doing his laundry. The Shark just twisted his pinkie rings and laughed at him.

"You're a goddamned drunk," the Shark said, picking up an empty beer can. "You live in a fucking garage! Look here, crackhead," he added, "don't ever call your father or me again."

That was two days before Wednesday, the day before Thanksgiving, today. As I pulled into Jack's driveway with a case of cigarettes and towing a pallet of Golden's beer on a trailer I heard a hard thump against the side of my rig. I got out. A golf ball whizzed by my head. Nicky was on his practice tee. I walked across the front lawn to say hello.

Tiger was straining at his leash and growled as I approached. The sun was setting like an empire, and Tiger's eyes glowed red reflecting the western sky. I pulled a can of beer from my bag and rolled it to him.

Nicky had the driver out and was warming up. I broke us each off a beer. We drank. He set another shag ball on the tee and ripped a line drive. It bounced off the St. Ignatius church down the block, just below the steeple.

"Keep your foot flat on the backswing," I said, "and don't lean in."

"This fucking slice is making me mad!" he said, pounding the club on the ground.

He set up another shot. He kept his foot flat, but leaned in. It flew straighter, banging on the large wooden doors guarding the entrance of St. Ignatius.

"I liked that a little better," he said.

It was Wednesday night and the place was full. We could hear them singing. The stained glass glowed warm in the chill of the evening.

Tiger had started to chew the aluminum can, and blood dripped from his mouth. Nicky finished his beer. I handed him another.

"You'll be at par in no time," I said.

"I'm only two shots off," he said. "Played my boss last weekend and nearly beat his ass, but the fucker kicked his ball out of the rough on Seventeen. I should have driven him into the ground like a goddamn tee. I get another chance tomorrow."

He set his last ball down.

"I bought a fat turkey for tomorrow," I said. "Bring your boss."

"We've got an early tee time, but I'll see what I can do."

Nicky executed a perfect swing. The ball arced gracefully into the air, long and proud. As it came down, thirty feet above the ground, it crashed through the largest stained glass window of St. Ignatius.

The praise inside stopped, and the congregated, god-fearing people of St. Ignatius unknowingly wet their pants. Shattered glass held onto the frame for a lifetime of a moment, then fell completely out. A hot, white light burned from inside the church. The faithful ran from the church in terror, down the street as if their clothes were on fire. Nicky bagged his driver.

"Well, I'm outta balls," he said. "No offense. Let's go, T."

I stepped onto the front porch of what was soon to be my house. I had not jumped the fence in months. One of my cel phones rang. It was the Veronica Phone.

"Hey, baby," she said, "what're you doing?"

"I'm walking through the front door."

"Oooh, the threshold," she said. "You're not carrying anyone arc you?"

"I bear only my sins."

I set down the beer and cigarettes.

"You know you make me hot when you talk like that. Why don't you come over here and whisper your sins in my ear."

She was rhyming on purpose. I could hear Cosmo in the background.

"Fish tacos, Veronica, fish tacos!" he insisted. "Where's the peanut butter, be-atch?

He was baiting me.

"And bring me back some cigarettes and a paper," he continued, "and the peanut butter, don't forget the peanut butter!"

"Veronica's not here," I said.

"Duh," she said. "Just come over."

"I can't," I said. "I've got a thawed turkey full of stuffing and other food to prepare for tomorrow. You come over here."

"Baby you know I'd love to come over and choke your turkey neck, but my mother is cooking and I have to go over there. I do have an extra pumpkin pie. Maybe I'll bring it over right now for our early Thanksgiving dessert."

The house was dark. I heard a motion in the kitchen. It sounded like Tipsy was into the garbage can. I moved slowly across the living room and peered around the corner. I could make out a dark figure on the ground moving slowly back and forth like a worm. The worm man was right, the worms are coming, I thought, they're here.

"Are you still there, Mudd?" Veronica asked.

The signal was breaking up, and her voice cut in and out. I flipped the light on.

In the middle of the kitchen floor Francois had his pants down and was fucking the stuffed Thanksgiving turkey like a farmhand from hell. The cold bird was splayed out in a missionary position, its fat drumsticks riding the air. Francois turned to me when the light came on. He began to frown and fuck harder.

"What are you doing, Mudd?" Veronica asked.

"I think I'm watching Francois fuck the turkey."

Francois was pumping furiously, like he was beating eggs for a quiche. He grabbed the turkey with both hands, and really gave it to that dead bird good.

"What makes you think that?" Veronica asked. "Wait, it sounded like you said Francois is a fucking beef jerky."

I hadn't blinked since I saw Francois.

"That's definitely what I'm watching," I concluded.

Francois' legs began to quiver. He slapped the bird's slippery, fat breast, muttering something in French.

"Well, I'm coming over with that pie. Get ready to get your whipped cream on," Veronica said, just before she hung up.

Francois' eyes rolled back in his head. His hips stopped

pumping. He had finished. He tried to stand, but slipped on a spot of turkey grease and fell on his face. He tried again. He was not smiling. Stuffing clung to his Gallic, and now softening, penis.

"Oui!" he declared, "I have fuck-ed your fat baird, Monsieur Liberte!" He pulled up his pants. "How aire all your dollar balls now?" He tightened his belt and ran his fingers through his hair. He pointed to himself and then to me. "I have express-ed to you, Uncle Sammy. Oui!"

He grabbed the bottle of wine that was on the counter and sniffed the air at me. Then he pushed past, leaving a trail of stuffing out the door to the garage.

I picked up the turkey. I washed the hair and dust from the floor off the breast. Then I filled the hole in the middle with extra stuffing, and put it all back in the fridge. He must have started at one end of the room because there was a trail of fowlish grease six feet long. I wiped the floor and cracked a fresh beer. Time to practice my art. I went down the hall to my new room.

The light was already on. I closed the door. Someone grabbed me from behind and threw me on the mattress. I looked up. It was Carmen. There was a burning cigarette in her hand, and she was gargling whiskey from a gallon jug as she stood over me. She swayed drunkenly, but the popeye stared directly at me.

"Carmen," I said, "you're here."

She moved toward me.

"I've come to a decision," she said, sliding out of the shadows.

"I've noticed," I said.

She was at the foot of the mattress and took a long pull on the whiskey. She pointed at me with the fingers that held the cigarette.

"You are going to be the father of my child," she said.

"Oui?" I said.

She reached out and lifted my chin with her hand.

"But you're not going to take your pants off," she said.

"Oui, oui?"

"And you need to wear this," she said, pulling a leash and collar out from behind where it was hung on her belt.

"No," I said.

"Oui!" she insisted.

She pushed my shoulder blades down on the mattress and climbed on top. She strapped on the collar, pulled the leash tight, and began to grind. Her head was thrown to the side, and she rode me like an upside-down horse.

I figured I could get in a quick rehearsal while she worked. I reached for STIFFY. I ran through a few major scales, then began the first verse of 'She's Always A Woman.' Carmen poured whiskey on me as I played. I lapped at it like a dog drinking falling November rain.

"Need some more motivation, huh?" she said after a few minutes. She pulled off her shirt. I stared at her brassiered breasts as they hove back and forth in front of my face. I was six weeks old again. I could smell her sex. I reached up to feel them. She slapped my hands away.

"No touch," she said. "You can't have me."

She pulled on the leash and the collar got tighter. Her torso was covered in tattoos of every color. I stared. I was being dry humped by a billboard from the Vegas Strip. I put the comb down and concentrated. I was getting close, ready to take care of business. There was a knock at the door.

"Coming," I said.

It was Veronica. She stood in the doorway holding a slightly steaming pumpkin pie. I was pinned and leashed, and couldn't get up to give her a hug.

"Looks like you already got your fucking dessert," Veronica implied.

"He's sweet too," Carmen said, still grinding. "Wanna join us?"

"Fuck you, whorecat! Star-fucker! Star-fucker! I hate you!" Veronica screamed.

She dug into the pie with her hand, scooping out a handful of filling.

"You like pie, bitch?"

She hurled it at Carmen's head. Carmen twisted like Medusa and the pie missed, hitting me square in the face. Carmen laughed. Veronica dug the rest of the pie and flung it at me. She finally whipped the pie tin and it bounced off Carmen's head. Carmen flicked her cigarette butt at

Veronica. I had pie in my eyes so I didn't see Veronica as she slammed the door on her way out.

"Alright, kid," Carmen said, "it's just you and me now."

With the pie in my eyes it was dark. I needed some whipped cream. Then I imagined I was fucking a stuffed turkey, the warm softness of the stuffing, the slippery breast to grapple with. I imagined my turkey in the finest lingerie stripping only for me.

With Carmen humping and the turkey fantasy I came right away. Carmen reached into her bag and pulled out a test tube. She popped the cap and scraped the tube along the inside of my pants, collecting my half of our future child from a cold, sticky and near certain death. Then she zipped me up and undid my collar.

"You've made an enormous contribution to humanity today," she said. "With your wealth and my vision our child will be one of the most powerful people on the planet." She stuffed the tube in her bag. "Adios, Papi," she said, taking a swig from the bottle and letting herself out.

"Sayonara, my Josephine," I bid.

There was pie everywhere. I wiped the glob out of my eyes and ate it. I grabbed a hundred-dollar bill and wiped the inside of my pants clean. The house was quiet, except for Yves Montand groaning away at the night in the echo of the garage.

I sat up to light a cigarette. The whiskey that Carmen had poured on me was not fully dry, and when I struck the lighter there was a sudden blue flash. It lasted only a second but it was enough to remove my eyebrows. The room filled with the stink of singed hair. I changed out of the whiskey and semen soaked clothes, then lit my smoke. Come the morn we would give thanks.

Rap 32

THANKSGIVING MORNING. I checked the turkey in the oven. It was done. The members of the house sat around the table as a family. Diane was there. She was Jack's fiancée.

"You look good without eyebrows," she told me.

The table was set. Yams, cranberry sauce, wine, corn, wine, biscuits, wine, gravy, wine, butter, and the stuffed turkey in the middle. Francois sat directly across from me, the turkey between us. He hadn't spoken to anyone all morning. He reached under the table and adjusted his biscotti.

"Who wants to cut the turkey?" Jack asked.

Francois stood and smacked the table with his palm.

"I do not fuck ze tairkey!" he proclaimed.

For a moment he was Roman Polanski. Nobody said anything. Francois slowly sat back down.

"Okay," Jack said, "I'll carve the turkey."

There was a football game on the television. A large man was being carried off the field on a stretcher. The crowd was cheering and throwing cups of beer at him as they loaded him into the ambulance. Jack finished carving and sat down.

"Who wants to say grace?" Diane asked.

Nobody said anything.

"Okay," she said, "fuck it. Let's eat."

Francois and I immediately reached for the drumsticks. We ripped them both off hard before anyone else lifted a fork. Potatoes were passed, biscuits and cranberry sauce. Jack offered me the bowl of stuffing. I passed it to Francois. He diligently and silently passed it to Diane, glaring at me in French as he did. I poured gravy on my drumstick.

"What, you guys don't like stuffing?" Diane asked. "I love stuffing." She took two large spoonfuls.

Francois watched me. The doorbell rang.

It was Nicky. He stood in the doorway dressed in plaid knickers and a knit cap with a fuzzy white ball on top. He had an empty wine glass in one hand and a nine-iron in the other.

"I beat my boss, that fuckin' dog catchin' bitch," Nicky said. "He now owes me a raise. I got it in writing," he added, showing me a notarized letter.

I saw Tiger behind him. He was dressed in knit plaid like Nicky, only the fuzzy ball on his cap was black.

"Do you mind if my animal ambassador comes too?"

Nicky asked.

Before I could answer Tiger broke free and charged inside. He went straight for the table, whipping the leash behind him. He jumped for the turkey, but Jack intercepted him in midair. The Miniature Pinscher was snapping his fangs like a knitted wolverine. Nicky tied the leash to the bottom of the couch.

"Nicky, this is my fiancée, Diane," Jack said.

"Hey, just like that song," Nicky said.

"You're a 100 watt bulb," Jack said.

Diane's plate had been spilled in the commotion. Nicky sat down and loaded up.

"This isn't that fake fucking stuffing, is it?" Nicky asked, scooping.

"It's the real deal," I said.

Nicky took the remainder of the stuffing and began shoveling it into his mouth.

"It's good," he said, "but it's a little chewy."

Tiger was a firecracker. I poured some wine in a dish and he drank it down. Jack and Diane finished cleaning the mess he had made leaping for the turkey. She loaded her plate again, minus stuffing.

Tipsy had watched it all from the corner. He shook his head in disgust, then approached Tiger as if he had no other choice. The dogs circled each other in challenge.

"Ruff? Rrruff-ruff," Tiger said.

"Grrr? Ruff-grrr!" Tipsy said. "Rufff-ruff!"

"Ruff me?" Tiger said. "Ruff you!"

Tipsy felt strongly enough about it all to share his nuts with Tiger's nose. With a head full of wine Tiger bit down brusquely on Tipsy's dangling sack. It was over before it started. Tipsy had no chance. Jack and Nicky separated them. The house phone rang. I answered it.

"Your bitch is a turkey!" the voice screamed.

"It's for you," I said to Francois. Then I recognized Veronica's voice. I hung up.

Dinner was over. We went to the living room. Tipsy watched Tiger from the corner. Jack went around pouring wine. Nicky held out his glass. Jack poured.

"Ze glass you hold here," Francois told Nicky, pointing

to the stem. "Et es no football."

"I've had four glasses already, St. Francis," Nicky said.

Francois told Nicky his name was Francois.

"All I'm worried about is getting the wine to my fucking mouth," Nicky concluded.

The day needed a fresh pack of cigarettes. I went to the freezer. There were twenty cartons stuffed in, just chillin'. I pulled one out, ripped it open, cracked and crumpled the cellophane in thanks, packed it, opened the box and banged a cigarette out. I lit it. The Veronica Phone vibrated.

"Don't hang up on me!" she said, just before hanging up.

I puffed out a cloud of smoke. The doorbell rang. Someone was pounding on the screen door. The dogs began barking.

"Let me in, motherfuckers!"

Then insane cackling, like a barnyard party. It was Carmen. I let her in. She was wearing a torn backpack and had a highball tumbler in hand. She slipped on the doormat and cursed, but didn't spill her drink. She threw her arms around me.

"How's the future ruler of the world?" she breathed in my ear.

Tiger was nipping savagely at Carmen's leg. She pulled a bottle from her bag and poured his dish full of scotch. He lapped it up, neat.

"A little scotch for the golfer," Carmen said.

"Hey, don't be givin' him that shit!" Nicky shouted, coming across the room.

He pulled the bowl from Tiger and poured the scotch into his own glass. Carmen stood up straight and gave him the stink-eye with her pop.

"And just who the fuck are you?" Carmen wondered, looking around for answers, then squinting at Nicky. "Oh," she realized, "I see it doesn't matter."

She turned back to me. "Just sold another painting. Ten grand this time."

Francois sniffed the air with impoverished disgust. Carmen rolled into a chair at the end of the room and pulled out a fat joint. She lit it and filled her glass with scotch.

There was a halftime commercial on the television. A

sharp-dressed woman in high heels was walking her dog down the sidewalk, spraying perfume on everyone. She sprayed an old vegetable peddler in the face, and he smiled as if she were his daughter.

"Peanut butter," Nicky said.

"No, thanks," I said.

Nicky continued.

"You know how you see those women walking down the street with their dogs, and you see those big smiles on their faces? The night before they film the commercial they put peanut butter on their pussies and got those dogs lickin' their pussies every night. If I had a pussy I'd be doin' it every goddamn night."

"What the fuck did you just say?" Carmen asked, sniffing the air. "That smelled like a load of bullshit."

I puffed the joint and passed it. They were both drunk and stunk. Carmen put her glass down. Nicky peered at her. The dogs watched silently.

"I said," Nicky said, "it looks like you need to wax your board."

"I know you didn't just say that. What the fuck does that mean? Explain it to me," Carmen said, bristling from the hatred and the drink.

Nicky stood and approached her.

"This is what the fuck it means."

He reached for the back of her neck where an herb garden of hairs climbed out of her shirt. He plucked a few and showed them to her, then rubbed his fingers together until they all fell like petals. Nicky threw his head back and laughed, and the knit ball on his beanie bounced around.

"Save the rainforest, bitch," Carmen said, standing to face him, dusting off her knuckles. "I think you need to take a breathalyzer, motherfucker, 'cause you don't know what the fuck you're talking about. Shit," she said, looking around in mock penitence, "I shouldn't even be talking to you."

The air was dense, thick with the tension of pain and scotch tinged with cigarette smoke. The pilgrims had not progressed. It was the Nineteenth Hole gone bad. No one spoke. The doorbell rang.

"I'll get it," I said.

On the porch was a group of ten or fifteen sorority sisters. The girl in front leaned over to her friend.

"See," she said, "I told you it was him." Then to me. "We saw you at the store a few days ago and followed you home. I know it's Thanksgiving and all, but do you want to come out and party with us?"

I looked at Carmen and Nicky. They were still squared off like right angles.

"We've got some weed," she added.

"Come in," I said, opening the door.

The party raged for hours. More people arrived. Cigarette butts were extinguished on the floor. In the bathroom an exchange student named Olaf was doing an upside down beer bong in a tub full of water. At one point Diane leaned over and stuck her tongue down my throat when Jack wasn't looking.

"You're an animal," I said.

Everyone wanted a piece of me.

"Take your hands off me," I said.

"Save it for later," she said, walking away.

The loud music had separated Nicky and Carmen. Tiger was getting wasted, humping all over a hottie pink Bichon Frise. Tipsy told Jack that Tiger had cock-blocked him, hardcore. The Bichon had laughed at Tipsy. Now Tipsy was no longer the alpha and sat against the wall, a dogged lover, not a fighter, a four-legged, wet-nosed nerd.

In a shock the front window shattered as something was hurled through it from outside. The object rolled to a stop in the middle of the living room. It was Mojo, returning like a Jedi. I looked out the door. Veronica was on the sidewalk. She flipped me the two-fisted bird.

"Eat shit and die, writer!" she hollered. Then she ran up onto the lawn and kicked the surfboard, but it didn't budge.

Porch lights were turned on. Someone behind me snarled, and a squad of fanatics pushed past and chased Veronica up the street. I lit a cigarette and went back inside.

"Play a song for us," a small crowd pleaded.

I obliged and pulled out STIFFY.

"Ooooooo," the crowd said when it saw the jar of blue disinfectant.

In a linty-eyed moment of irony I got things working with the overture from *The Barber of Seville*. I seconded the motion with 'My Way'. Olaf was in the front row.

"That song always makes me..." he cried, "...makes me..." he cried again, "...makes me..." he cried a final time, "...cry!" he cried.

Francois was blubbering and drunk, and pushed his way past Olaf to the front of the crowd. He reached out and grabbed the instrument from my hand.

"Ze comb, et es mine!" he said. "Ze comb I drop-ped at ze gallaree!"

He put the comb to his mouth but only drooled. The crowd booed. He staggered backwards.

Nicky entered the scene also staggering backwards. He was drunk and horny and yelling some sexual affirmation to one of the sorority sisters as she followed him through the crowd. Nicky bumped into Francois. When he turned around his eyes locked on STIFFY.

"Gimmee that, Francis, you pussy," Nicky said, grabbing STIFFY from Francois. "When you comb your bush you hold ze comb here."

Nicky mocked Francois holding a wine glass by the stem, then jammed STIFFY down his knickers and began combing his pubes. He made a face as he hit a snag, then straightened it out. "Much better," he said, handing the comb back to Francois, smirking and confident.

The room stood still as an empty bowling alley. From the crowd Carmen lunged at Nicky's head, knocking him to the ground. Fists were flying. Carmen kneed him in his crotch and Nicky made a strange, non-phonetic sound. Carmen pushed him out the front door and followed him into the yard.

"I'm gonna feed you your own tongue!" she promised.

She began throttling him, but he made a reverse move and they rolled around on the grass. Soon Nicky was on top, slamming her head down in the grass.

"Somebody bring me the peanut butter!" he yelled. "How you like my breath now?" Nicky wondered aloud, spitting a wad of blood into her face.

"I still hate it, punk," she admitted through gritted teeth.

Carmen mustered her strength and flipped Nicky onto his back. She gathered one of his legs and brought it to his head and bounced him around like that for a while. The crowd cheered like Centurions. She kidney-punched him a few times then got him in a sleeper hold.

"This is what we do to little boys who don't behave," she said. She ripped off his plaid knickers with one hand and began spanking him. The slapping sound echoed off the houses, and the neighbors who had stepped out to watch covered their faces and pointed.

"Who's your Momma?" Carmen said. Nicky was crying now like a candyless orphan. "Who's your Momma!" Carmen repeated.

"You are," Nicky said, sniveling and bloody.

"Goddamn right," she said, kicking him home, pantless and defeated. She picked up the garden hose and sprayed him down as he ran away. Tiger had broken loose during the melee and ran after Nicky.

I returned to the house. Francois was still holding STIFFY. Nicky's curlicue hairs were stiff and locked forever on the teeth. He handed the comb to me.

"You keep ze comb, Mudds. My geeft to you." He patted me on the shoulder, and resigned himself to the garage for the remainder of the evening.

The house looked like the turkey, stripped and masticated. Nothing but a hollow shell of skeleton left. I looked at STIFFY in my hand.

"That's the most fun I had at a party in a long time," Carmen said, brushing the dirt off her pants.

The rest of the crowd wandered off into the night. Tipsy was on the table scavenging leftovers. I went to the fridge. One beer left, laying on its side. The night was old. I turned off the lights. I sat on the couch and watched the streetlight flicker through the smashed front window. The stars were shining, somewhere, but I could not see them.

Rap 33

IT WAS HOT FOR DECEMBER. The cardboard dust in the warehouse turned the sweat on my skin to glue.

I had lost the Grail and was sent back to the rock pile. They had taken it all. The large vehicle shaped like an athletic shoe, the cel phones, even the Veronica Phone, the credit cards, everything except the freezer full of cigarettes. Those would be gone soon as well.

After Nicky had groomed his bush with STIFFY the comb would not stay in tune. It always wanted to play half-notes flat. The curlicue hairs vibrated and tickled my nose. With a few nonchalant strokes it had become an accursed artifact.

I bought another comb. It was not the same. I could not hold a note or carry a tune without STIFFY. I could only make raspberry sounds as the drool lilted down my chin. My friends of two months treated me like a bill collector. I tried other devices, hairbrushes and various kitchen utensils. I even tried strapping some toilet paper across the tongs of the wishbone after Thanksgiving. I was suddenly a musical dunce, a fluteless Pan, a luteless lute player, creatively lobotomized by fate.

"Sorry, babe," the Vice President of the label said. "If you can't play, we can't pay."

It all blew away like an autistic brainstorm. Plus, I owed what I had already spent. Which meant one thing - back to work.

It was hot for December. Mr. McMack, the owner of the warehouse, was scheduled to arrive late in the morning. Jerry was scampering about, making preparations. Tom approached me, sweating and smiling.

"Well, well, well," he said, "look who's not ready to get on with his life. Come with me, Sir."

The desk was still down the aisle where I had left it months before, all five-hundred pounds of it. I had grown weak in my celebrity. My star had drained into a black hole and I felt like a rock. I was a rock star without the star. The game went on.

Carmen had another partner for deliveries. We smoked

on the morning break.

"No offense," she said, "but I sold your sperm to a friend for four-hundred dollars."

I sipped my coffee.

"She said she didn't care if you were rich and powerful or not."

I pulled on my cig and blew a perfect smoke ring.

"I even helped her inseminate," Carmen said.

I watched my smoke ring expand into the air. Its whiteness turned to gray, and then disappeared.

"Oh well," she said, "gotta get back to work. See ya round, buddy."

I finished my coffee. The sugar had descended into a lump at the bottom of the cup. I ashed my smoke into the sugar. Dale drove by on the forklift and honked.

"The owner's on his way in," he said. "Supposed to be bringing his daughter to survey the working class."

I picked up a broom and began pushing dust together in a neat pile. A limousine pulled up next to the loading dock and honked. Jerry ran down the steps and opened the door. A well dressed man stepped out. It was Mr. McMack. He shot his cuffs at Jerry.

"Yes, Sir," Jerry said.

Mr. McMack's tie clasp twinkled in the sunlight. He reached into the limo and helped his daughter out.

"Yes, Sir," Jerry said again, even though the owner had said nothing.

Mr. McMack lit the stub of his cigar while Jerry opened an umbrella over him and his daughter. The three of them strolled into the warehouse in the shade. They stopped ten feet short of where I was sweeping.

The young Miss McMack carved a striking figure out of the solemn drudgery of the warehouse. She stood next to her father, twisting in place as innocent as a sunflower.

"I brought Candy down to see what life will be like once she graduates from the University in June," Mr. McMack said.

"Yes, Sir," Jerry said.

Candy twirled her purse strap between her fingers. I watched her from the side as she surveyed the hot, sweating, sleeveless men bending and lifting heavy objects.

"Even though she's graduating from law school she should still recognize the hard work and suffering that made me the man I am today," McMack continued.

"Of course, Sir," Jerry said.

Candy was wearing a thin, tight fitting blouse, and her mother had endowed her with a pair of not unlarge breasts. I stared at her as she watched the men load the trucks. As her breasts heaved up and down in the heat her nipples began to push up from the fabric. They pushed higher. And higher. And higher, until I was sure they would rip through her blouse. Her knees were rubbing together slowly. She arched her back as her father pointed around with his cigar.

I don't know how long I was staring at her breasts. I had been pushing the broom the entire time and now a large cloud of dust had risen. I was gripping the handle tight and my palms were certainly beginning to sweat. The dust cloud moved slower than the Great Depression toward Jerry and the McMacks. There was a tap on my shoulder. It was Tom.

"Come with me, Young Mudd," he said. "I have a better job for your broom."

I barely heard him. I couldn't break my eyes from her trust funds. I stood pushing more dust from the ground into the air, and the cloud floated closer to their heads. Tom grabbed my arm and pulled me outside. As we rounded the corner I could hear Jerry and the McMacks choking and coughing on the cloud of dust.

Tom took me around the building to the dumpster. Trash was thrown everywhere. Bags were torn open and three day old coffee grounds were steaming on the ground in the morning sun. A bum had taken a shit while leaning on the dumpster and left a vodka bottle next to it. Someone had puked. I looked at the broom in my hands. Tom looked at the broom. He walked away laughing.

I approached the dumpster and began sweeping. I picked up the vodka bottle to see if they had left any for me. The wind shifted directions and I smelled a half-eaten liverwurst sandwich that was covered in flies. My eyes watered and I barfed. The wind shifted again and I got a different smell. This one was sweet, familiar. I wondered if Carmen had her flask with her. Some whiskey would freshen my breath. I pulled out a cigarette and lit up.

As I stood by the dumpster with my smoke the sweet familiar smell came again. I turned and looked inside. It grew stronger. I went through several bags of trash. It touched something deep inside me, but I couldn't put it into words. It seemed out of context. Then I made the discovery.

Deep in the trash, inside two dark plastic bags, wrapped in aluminum foil were two bales of highly compressed, stinky and sticky, skunkweed marijuana. They must have weighed twenty pounds each. I made a quick pipe from an edge of the foil and stuffed a bud in. It tasted like the first time. I wrapped the bale and covered it. I went in and found Dale.

"I need your help with something," I said.

He left the forklift and followed me out.

"Must be a drop for some dealers," he said. "Nice, out of the way dumpster. They'll probably be coming tonight to pick it up." I passed him the foil pipe with a fresh pack. "Too bad it won't be here," he added.

I finished cleaning around the dumpster. Dale went back to work. The McMacks left in their limo, gilded eyebrows and law school hair covered in warehouse dust.

Five o'clock arrived. Dale and I drove around after we clocked out to make sure everyone had gone home. When the parking lot was clear we raided the stash. It was getting dark and the halogen bulb flickered on above us. I shoved one bale into my backpack. It barely fit. We smoked fresh bowls on the way to the house.

Rap 34

THREE BLOCKS FROM HOME we stopped for a light.

"Looks like we're not the only lucky bastards today," Dale said, pointing to the car next to us.

In the lights of the intersection there was a woman giving a blow job to the guy driving. I looked closer. The guy was

Ted. He seemed to be enjoying it quite a bit. The woman was naked, and as she got more into it her ass raised up and pressed against the window. That ass looked familiar, like the smell of the bales in the dumpster, but I couldn't place it. It, too, was out of context.

The ass lowered and Ted looked mildly satisfied. Then the woman climbed on his dick and began humping him wildly. As she swung her head back and forth a ray of light caught her features. It was Veronica. Of course, I thought, that's where I'd seen that ass before.

Ted's car was rocking now. The light had changed and people were honking at us. Just before we pulled away Veronica noticed us watching. She smiled at me then flipped me off. Ted saw me and winked. He peeled out, leaving us in a cloud of burnt rubber.

My mouth was dry so I asked Dale to drop me at a store for a sixpack. I walked the rest of the way home with a sagging backpack and a sixpack in my hand. I cracked one open along the way.

Francois was seated on the couch when I walked in. He was now civil as a citizen to me. Once I was dirt poor and destitute again he apologized for screwing the turkey. My poverty regained had also moved me back to my home on the range, the garage, which seemed to give him a minor satisfaction.

He was watching television wide-eyed and shuddering in his seat. He was holding a cup of coffee, and it was spilling on his pants as his arm vibrated.

"You're shaking," I said.

"I em gone from ze hash," he said. "I em driving to crazee." His other hand was holding a cigarette. The ash shook loose onto the arm of the couch. His nose perked up. "What is ze smell? I know eet."

I pulled off my pack. I broke as much off as I could hold in one hand, about two ounces, and handed it to him.

"Zank you, Mudds," he said.

He had a joint rolled and lit before I left the room. When I returned with a fresh beer ten minutes later he was passed out. The window was still boarded up where Veronica had thrown Mojo through. There would not even be a breeze to blow in. I sat in a chair and felt the day slip away like a cat in the night.

Rap 35

I WOKE UP AND CALLED THE WAREHOUSE to tell them I would not be coming in.

"One more time and you're fired," Jerry said. "Hope you feel better."

Robbed of musical skills I sat once again at the typewriter. I wrote a few quick sentences. I walked around the house. I wrote a few more. I did some pushups. My work was done for the day. I reached in the backpack, pulled out a bud and smoked.

My ears were bent for the tolling bells of Miguel's ice cream truck. He would certainly take the bale off my hands at a reasonable price. The weed would sell itself. It was a sure thing.

I would wait no more. Early in the afternoon the merry strains of 'Pop Goes The Weasel' drifted over the electrical din of the freeway. I put on my best shirt and hoisted the pack over my shoulder. I walked light on my feet.

Miguel was parked at the far end of the block. I moved fast, but one of my shoes came untied. I bent over and pulled, but the lace was old and rotten and snapped off in my hand. I relaced it, but it broke a second time.

As I was bent to my knees an ill wind bristled my ear hairs, and I cut my head around. I sensed the ghastly power of eyes watching me. I looked left, then right. It felt as though the Shrouded Rider was approaching, but something else was on its way.

The sprinkler-heads on the lawn surrounding me chugged suddenly to life. I bolted forward, stopping just past the sprinklers, one shoe flapping. In the brief shower I was nearly soaked. It was reclaimed water, and now I smelled like an overflowing public toilet.

My backpack was waterproof. The investment was

saved, but my shoelace was finished. Rather than flop it down the street I kicked off the whole shoe. My walk was that of a man who had lost three inches of leg bone. Up and down, step after step without the shoe. Miguel's engine started and he pulled away.

I began running, my soaked clothing slapping hard against my body. He was driving slow enough that I could not lose him, and fast enough that I could not catch him. I stubbed my bare toe on a concrete curb and almost went down. He stopped at the end of the next block and parked in front of the Evening Wood Nursing Home.

My ears were ringing from the excitement. The bottom of my bare foot burned and I panted enormously. I reached Miguel's window, but there were already two people from Evening Wood in line.

The smirking kid in front of me was wearing a hairnet and kitchen scrubs that had the name "McTuggins" written on them in black ink. The lady at the window was a nurse. She thanked Miguel and turned with a medicine cup containing one honking big white pill.

McTuggins reached for the pill as she walked past. The nurse slapped his hand.

"Get yer paws off," she scolded, "you know this ain't for you."

The nurse stepped across a small lawn to Evening Wood's cafeteria patio. Sitting there was the expressionless old man with the shock of white hair. He was in a rocking chair dowsed in the shadows of the porch. He had watched me fall on my face months ago, and now, as the reclaimed water dripped from my hair into my face, and then onto my shoeless right foot, he was watching me again. No laughter. Nothing. He was the Shrouded Rocker that did not rock.

He was sitting there when the nurse walked up. She said something to him, but he did not even ignore her. The nurse put one hand on her hip, and held the medicine cup in front of his face. He didn't give a rat's ass. He was glacial.

She shrugged and feigned to walk away. The password was abandonment. His jaw dropped open. The nurse took the pill between her thumb and index finger and aimed carefully. She popped the pill into his mouth from across the patio, then chased it with a squirt of water from a plastic bottle. His mouth closed and he swallowed without a gulp. He still stared straight ahead, never flinching, not a hint of gag, like a pill machine or a tin penny bank.

McTuggins turned and left Miguel's window with a brown bag wrapped around a bottle.

"Lunch time is punch time," he said, before drinking hard from the bottle. Some punch escaped the corners of his mouth. He lifted the overturned bottle above his head and poured the rest over his face, then threw the empty bottle on the lawn in front of the white-haired old man. He rubbed the punch into the skin of his face, then began dancing around in glee.

"Fuck, fucking, yeah!" he yelled.

"McTuggins, get your ass back in here!"

It was the cook.

"What you think this is, some kind of circus parade?"

She was waving a spatula at him from the door of the cafeteria.

"Goddamn, I love California!" he yelled. He pumped his fist in the air and did a somersault on his way back to the kitchen.

Miguel smiled at me from the truck.

"My friend, I have not seen you for so long. How are you?"

Seeing the old man again had sent a chill through my scrotum. The ill wind bristled my ear hairs. I looked under Miguel's truck, then scanned the other side of the street. Only the bone-dry wind. It was undeniable. No one.

"You are anxious, my friend," he said. "For that I have somethееng."

I heard the rattle of what sounded like candy in a jar. He produced a proud blue pill the size of my thumbnail, and handed me a cup of water. I swallowed too fast, and gagged on the hunk of medicine. More water. Finally I was able to speak.

"I want to make you an offer you can't refuse," I said.

"Si," he said, "I can smell your offer from here. You go to the back."

He let me in the back of the truck. I showed him the bale.

He offered me ten-thousand dollars. I said I would take it. He opened the lid of a freezer built into the side of the truck. Ice vapors rose and engulfed his head as he reached deep into the vault. When he stood his moustache was covered in frost. He smiled.

"Thees ees what we call cold, hard cash," he said, heaving a gruff, wheezing laugh. He handed me a stack of crisp, frozen one-hundred dollar bills. They were still steaming. He opened another freezer and stuffed the bale inside.

"Now, my friend, we dreenk to our beesnuss together," he said.

He pulled from behind him on a shelf an oven-fired mud jug. It was corked with a piece of bark. He poured us each a glass.

"Thees dreenk," he whispered, "eet ees better than El Pulque."

I remembered the pulque. I had to like it. I drank it down. It was like sugar water. He drank his and poured us another.

I began to feel relaxed. After my afternoon jog, the loss of my shoe and public shower in the treated wastewater, my senses were tight. Now they began to lift. Miguel poured me another of the mystery elixir. We sang narcocorridos and drank to ourselves in the back of his truck.

"Thees ees from the sacred cactus," he said, holding his glass up so that it refracted the light coming in. "Only three men know where thees cactus ees. Eet ees gigante, a two-thousand year old saguaro. Eet holds the spirits of my ancestors, and theirs before them. Eet ees where God leeves."

God indeed. I finished my third and held the cup out for another.

"No, my friend. A man can only have three." He leaned forward. "Eef you take more, then you are to challenge God. Besides," he said, leaning back with a smile, "you do not feel heem all right away. You stay here."

Miguel started the truck and we pulled away. When he wasn't looking I poured a sip more of the cactus water, a mere shot, and whipped it back.

I remember setting the cup down and patting the frozen

ten-thousand in my pocket. I thought of having a smoke, but as I reached for my cigarettes the freezers began to rise off the deck, and I heard a strange whirling sound. For a moment I blacked out. When my eyes opened there was a smoking, three-foot steamroller bong floating in the air in front of me. Then I heard the voice.

"Listen to me closely, Mudd," the voice said, "this is God."

"I trust you already," I said.

The bong erupted in flames, and continued to burn without being consumed as it hovered.

"Don't patronize me, jag-off!" God said. "I have something very important to share with you. We don't have much time and I can't have you fucking this up, so pay attention!"

Kerouac had George Shearing, I got Cheech and Chong.

"Here's the deal," he said. "I need you to go forth and redeem the human race from sin. No one has seen the last guy I sent, and no one knows where he is, probably off getting shitfaced down in Tijuana with that bumblefuck crew of beards he hooked up with."

"I can grow a beard," I said.

"Anyway," God continued, "the task has fallen to you. In exchange you will receive everlasting life in my eternal holy kingdom. Or, a set of steak knives, I can never keep the pay grades straight. Tell me, are you up to this task?"

"No one will believe me," I said.

"I knew it," God laughed, "I should have grabbed McTuggins. Quit crying you baby!"

I pulled out my cigarettes, but they were yanked from my hand by an invisible force. They floated there in front of me, then lightning shot out of the burning bong and began forging the pack into something different.

"Angels will be at your disposal," he continued, "and I've always got Augustine on speed dial if we need to bring in a ringer."

Sparks shot off my nose as the lightning arced across the truck. I could see that my cigarettes were being forged into a glowing rubber stamp.

"This stamp will be your validation," God said.

I reached out to touch it.

"Whoa there, Spartacus, it's not yours yet."

More lightning, this time engraving a wicked manual can opener on the stamp.

"There, now it's yours. This stamp will be your marker, but don't show it to anyone else. This is just between you and me, capeche? Oh, and don't lose it because, duh, it's one-of-a-kind."

The stamp dropped complete into my cupped hands. Miguel hit a speed bump and the truck bounced, flipping the stamp over in my hand. It was heavy. I held it up to the light.

"It's solid gold," I said.

"Just the handle." The bong leaned in. "What, you like gold?" he said, switching gears. "Yo, man, your lady like gold?"

In small puffs of smoke watches began appearing in the air in front of me, lining up as if on a jeweler's display case.

"Make me an offer, pick one you like, everyone needs a watch. I got necklaces, too."

It was a confluence of circumstances.

"If I have everlasting life I won't need a watch," I said.

"Fuckin' Rain Man over here! C'mon, I ain't throwin' no bricks against no penitentiary walls for nuthin'!" God paused. "Alright, forget the watch, I was only fooling."

The watches disappeared.

"Well, what do you say, Mudd? Cleanse the world of vice for me? I say again, are you up to this task? Will you trade your devotion to worldly pleasures for an everlasting soul?"

The back of the truck was silent.

"Well?" God said.

"Me?" I said.

"Mudd, you're a bitch to live with. Of course you! Who the fuck else would I be talking to?"

I felt the truck stop. There was silence. The burning bong floated.

"Well?!"

"Sure," I said.

"Fine, fine, m'boy. Look, don't fuck this up, Mudd. I got your number, and as you can see I'm almost cashed. Once

I'm gone, you'll be the last hope. Gimmee some bumps."

The end of the steamroller leaned in.

"Aw, don't leave me hangin', dog," he said.

I made a fist and gave God a bump.

"Aw, one more, dude, I may not see you again for a while," he said.

I gave God another bump.

"Now, go!" he commanded.

As the burning steamroller crackled into invisibility he added:

"And tell that dipshit neighbor of yours to stop fucking up my shit. He breaks another one of my windows and I take it out of his ass!"

I was still buzzing when Miguel dropped me off. My clothes had dried. I hadn't been on my feet for a while, and my legs danced like calamari under me.

"Vaya con dios, amigo," Miguel hollered. Then he wheezed and laughed as he stuffed a Havana in his mouth and drove off. Deep in my head I heard 'Pop Goes The Weasel' fade into the distance. I wavered on the sidewalk. I turned to see where I was.

I could see Manny's Market in the distance. I wasn't too far from home. I took a step, but realized the aftershocks of the cactus juice. It made the sidewalk feel like I was walking on water. The holy golden can opener stamp was still weighing heavy in my hand. I pocketed it, and taught myself to walk.

As I moved slowly forward I heard the flapping of large wings in the air behind me. I moved faster, but the wings got closer. I looked around as I walked.

Flying toward me was a huge rodent, a vile blonde rat with shredding teeth and wings made of tarpaper. I always recognized the Midnight Angel. Then I saw another, and another. It was my angel army, come to guide me. The angels made passes at my head, and I could feel the wind from their beating wings.

I looked up once more. The beasts were changing colors as they flew, first yellow, then a hideous bloody red which faded to green behind the snapping of their teeth, all swarming over me.

I felt a heavy splotch on my shoulder. I looked down. A sticky white spot with a green center was moist and full, like a sunny-side-up egg. Then another on my back. Angel shit. I felt a cloud of droppings brush my ear before smacking my neck. I reeled backward, tripped and began running. Manny's was half a block away. I hadn't been there since the robbery, but now I had no choice.

I made it to Manny's door. I was sweating and out of breath. The angels made their final reverent pass. They landed in formation on Manny's roof and in the surrounding palm trees.

As I stood still the building began to spin. I could feel my teeth grinding, and I tasted blood. With what little reason I had left I made it to the beer case for some light ale. That would straighten me out. I twisted the top off one and drank it dry. Manny watched me as I made my way to the register. I caught my reflection in a mirror. I was pale and soaked with sweat. I hobbled the last few steps.

I stood straight at the register. I set the beer on the counter and the room began to spin again. Then I saw the eyeball. It was the size of a skull, and floating above and behind Manny. The eyeball was laughing at me, cackling, whooping and wailing. Manny looked at me.

"Buddy, jou are fucked up," he said.

I did not argue. The eyeball was drawing near. I tasted a sample of heavy bile rising in my throat as I pulled the entire wad of now-melted money out of my pocket and set it on the counter. Then I puked all over Manny. I puked on the floating eyeball, and on the money. I puked on myself. Then I crumpled into a worthless, puking pile on the floor.

Rap 36

I WOKE UP ON A BENCH OF HARD CONCRETE. The air was cold. My best shirt was ruined, caked over with vomit and angel shit, and my right shoe was missing. I looked up. There was a huge steel door with a small square window. A mildewed, stainless steel toilet squatted across the room. A merciless bright light shined from high above. I was in the drunk tank.

My head was pounding. I sat up. My pants were wet.

"You pissed on yourself last night," someone said. He was a round man with a bald head. "When they brought you in you was talkin' some strange language," he said, "talkin' 'bout eyeballs and flyin' rats. Man, you was fucked up."

"Yes," I said, "so I've heard."

"Wish I could get hold of what you had," he said.

"The cactus is God," I said.

"Man, you still fucked up." He waved his hand at me and sat back. "Muthafucka talkin' 'bout God and shit."

There was a loud, dungeon-like sound. The door creaked open. Another drunk was shoved in. The door slammed behind him, and he swung around and began pounding on it.

"Easy, dude," Baldhead said, "you ain't gettin' outta here."

"I'm fucking innocent," the man said.

"Shee-it," Baldhead said, "you ain't innocent. You in here."

"Those cops lied! Now how I'm 'posed to get to work today?"

"Where you work at so important?" Baldhead asked.

The new man sat on the bench next to me.

"Sellin' beer at the stadium."

"They ain't gonna miss yo' ass," Baldhead laughed. "You just another beer man."

I thought of the stale, foamy beer smell of the stadium. I dry heaved in the corner.

"There's another innocent muthafucka," Baldhead said to the beer man, pointing at me.

A glob of drool fell from my bottom lip. I sat up. I felt in my pocket for the money, but it was gone. I felt in my other pocket for the solid gold can opener stamp. It was gone too. God was gonna be pissed.

"Hey, wait a minute," Baldhead said, leaning forward. "I reckonize you. You that dude on the cover of that magazine."

It took me a minute to realize he was speaking about me.

"Been there," I said, wiping my mouth, "done that."

The steel door echoed through the jail as it opened again.

"Alright boys," the guard said, "time for your tet shots."

He marched us out into the hall. There was a line of about twenty men waiting to get a shot from a nurse sitting at a table.

"This'z offensive bullshit," Baldhead said. "Ever time I'm in here they test me for this shit. I know I ain't got no tetanitusis."

We shuffled forward. A scuffle broke out at the head of the line. A man in an orange jumpsuit was arguing with the guards. He pushed one, so they clobbered him, cuffed him and dragged him down. He was yelling as they dragged him past.

"Has anyone seen my cel-phone? I want my lawyer! You can't do this to me!" He was flailing. "Don't let them stab you! Reptile fucks!" He grabbed my arm and looked me in the eye. "They want our blood for the Hills!"

Then he went down the line, engaging every inmate.

"Have you seen my cel-phone, brother?" he asked Baldhead behind me.

"Man, I fucked your cel-phone in the ass last night," Baldhead said.

"Find it!" he said to the inmate behind Baldhead, "I dropped it somewhere," he said to the next, "I think I left it in El Segundo, bro," to the next, until finally "Call me!" He put his fingers to his mouth and ear when he said this.

One of the guards smashed his wrist with a club. He howled like a cougar. "Don't let them take your humanity!" he shouted from down the hall. "You may be the only one left! Find my phone! Call..."

A huge steel door slammed and the hall was silent again.

"God told me the same thing," I said.

"All you muthafuckas crazy," Baldhead said, adding, "I did fuck his phone in the ass last night, that warn't no lie."

We shuffled along, following the bright yellow line down the hall. The walls were bare and white. I stunk of dried sweat and stale urine. I held out my arm for the nurse.

"This won't hurt," she promised.

It didn't.

Rap 37

I STOOD BEFORE THE JUDGE LATER THAT DAY.

"Mr. Mudd, since this is your first offense you are being released on your own recognizance. I order you to pay a fine of five hundred dollars within thirty days and attend six months of an alcohol abuse program of your choosing. I never want to see you before this bench again. Is this clear?"

"As glass," I said.

"Now," the judge said, "do you have anything you would like to say to the court?"

"Would the court have a cigarette?" I asked.

"No, Mr. Mudd," the judge boomed, "the court would not have a cigarette! Bailiff, take him away!"

They pushed me out into a glaring December sun and slammed the door behind me. I had been judged. Public drunkenness. I had been robbed. Ten thousand dollars and a holy golden stamp. I had been sentenced. Cash and rehab. I had fallen from grace.

I walked around the building to the plaza of the courthouse. There were more fountains than Rome, all bubbling over with the waters of justice. Flags blew in the breeze, and blindfolded, topless statues tempted the lawyers with their fecund, bronze breasts. I was getting a boner of freedom when a man approached me with a cigarette hanging from the corner of his mouth.

"Hey, buddy," he said, "you got a light?"

I told him I did not, then bummed a cigarette from him. He gave me two. I stuck one in my mouth.

I went to a phone to call someone to pick me up. No one was home. I looked to the sky for my army of angels. Not even a feather. I started the long walk home with the cigarette dangling from my lips.

A block away a woman with dark glasses and an extended cane was standing at a crosswalk. I waited behind her for the light to change. I saw a cloud of smoke erupt from her face. She was smoking.

"That cigarette sure smells good," I said.

"If you need a goddamn cigarette why don't you just say

so?" she said.

I lifted the cigarette in my lips.

"Just a light," I said.

"Oh," she said, "now he wants a light, too?"

"I thought you'd never ask," I said.

She turned and produced a palm-sized, scrollwork wooden matchbox.

I took one, then grabbed for a second.

"I don't think so," she said.

I put the second match back.

She smiled a smile of half disgust. I lit my cigarette. She didn't cross when the light changed. Three blocks away I looked back. She was still standing there smoking at the crossroads.

I removed my remaining shoe and tossed it in a trashcan, worthless without its pair. I was barefoot and walked all the way home a true pilgrim.

Rap 38

I MADE IT SOBER TO MY FIRST REHAB MEETING. I would give them a chance. It was held once a week in a cavernous old house under the flight path of jets taking off from the airport.

It was a men's meeting, sponsored by Milwaukee's Water non-alcoholic beer. There was a banner across the entrance. "It's later than you think," it read, "do something extra special with your life. We'll be here when you get back."

When I arrived there were already twenty or thirty guys out front. Everyone was smoking. Most held a drink of some kind, stainless steel travel mugs, disposable convenience store cups, water bottles. I could smell coffee brewing inside. I lit a cigarette and went in.

I had been sober for a week, since I had been in the tank. I poured a cup of coffee. I stood in the back corner. There was a tap on my shoulder.

"Pssst, move it buddy," the man said, pointing at the

place I was standing. "I've been standing here for nine years."

"This is my first time," I said.

"They're gonna make you share if you sit up front," he said, wincing.

There were rows of folding chairs facing a podium. I sat in the back of the room, three rows behind everyone else. I was there only a minute when a man carrying a travel case sauntered in, looked around and sat next to me.

"Am I late?" he asked. "Did I miss anything?"

"It's just starting," I said.

He gave me his pitch.

"The name's Dickey," he said, handing me his card. "Capital D, small i, small c, small k, small e, small y. Like an ascot. Small a, small s, small c, small o, small t, and tea is all that I'm totaling, my friend. Been sober a while now. I haven't seen you at this meeting before."

"I'm new to the crew," I said. "Small c, small r, small e, small w."

"Just quit, huh? Friend, I can tell ya I drank myself outta the real estate game, then I drank myself outta drinking. Brother, I was a dee-runk! Then, when I quit drinking, my therapist pointed out that I had all this time on my hands. Gotta do something," he reasoned, throwing his hands around, "or else I'd sit around all day marveling at how I had deceived myself with drink all those years."

"Man must do something to illustrate his bureaucracy," I said.

"You know, that's quite profound. Who said that?"

"I did," I said. "Didn't you recognize my voice?"

"I can tell you're a man of character," he noticed, slapping my knee. "You remind me of an uncle of mine in Ohio. I think he said something like that once, something like 'man is big on procedure'. His wife, my Aunt Kate, wonderful, dear, cherubic woman, made a mean blue-ribbon cherry pie. My uncle used to say that's why he married her. He was the philosopher, but Aunt Kate was a collector. She collected rubber stamps like it wasn't nobody's business, she had thousands."

"We might be related," I said.

"Really? We buried those stamps with her in the plot alongside. You know that phrase 'you can't take it with you'? She took it with her," he said, punctuating the modified aphorism with a nod. "Speaking of collecting, you'd sure have no trouble finding a collector in this room."

He pointed them out.

"There's the postcard collector, the coin collector, the sneaker collector, the comic book collector, and over there, that's the Captain," he said, pointing to a bearded sage in the corner. "He's the wife collector, but, ah, he never shows, only tells. They say he flew over a thousand combat missions in Vietnam, then flew 747s for twenty years. One night he sees some lights he can't explain at thirty-thousand feet, then poof! See ya later, good life." He shook his head. "Look at him there."

I looked at him there. He appeared courageous. I imagined wings on his back.

"There was also the rubber stamp collector," Dickey said. "He's just gone, don't ask, and damned if he wasn't my best customer."

Dickey opened his case.

"If you're wondering why I'm tellin' you all this," he said, "well, I'm telling you the truth. I never lie. Superman lies more than me."

I thought he would pull out the crown jewels. They were all on display, each rubber stamp sealed in plastic and priced. He was impatient and brash, a pretender to the throne, a rubber stamp hustler.

"I'll bet you're a man who's big on procedure," he mused. "Hot days, now I'm excited!"

He straightened his coat by pulling on both lapels, then began naming them all. There were happy stamps, business stamps, library stamps, camel-toe stamps, joke stamps, accounting stamps, theater stamps, domestic stamps, foreign stamps, passport stamps, railroad stamps and notary stamps. There was even one seal of approval. He gave me the hook.

"I'm here today to offer you the whole shebang at one low price."

Then I saw it. The pecker in the bush, the holy in the

grail. It was a stamp from the blue. The golden manual can opener stamp God had created and entrusted to me in the back of Miguel's truck. The golden manual can opener stamp I had lost and was now rediscovering at my first step of redemption. I had an inkling of a grand design. He held it up.

"This is a new one," he bragged. "I call it El Dorado because of its solid gold handle. It appears to be forged from the highest quality virgin Amazonian rubber, no record of production values, in mint condition. I found it in the beer case at a convenience store, of all places. What was it doing there? I couldn't believe it."

He lifted El Dorado up to catch the light. I reached out in awe for the voluptuous, vulcanized ingot.

"I saw it as a sign," he said, delicately keeping El Dorado just out of reach, "a sign to not sell this one. This one's for me." He placed El Dorado in his pocket. "Even though I could fetch a cool ten grand. I might even talk the right person into twelve." He looked around the room. "In my prime I coulda, woulda and shouda sold each one of these guys the Brooklyn Bridge, twice," he said. "You know, I sold Mamet the Glengarry estate? Now look at me."

I looked at him. He dressed like an upscale cab driver, and shaved about as often.

"That's what I love about coming to these meetings," he continued. "Not a single pipe dream in the room. These men have all taken charge of their destinies, even the Captain."

We both looked at the Captain. Someone cleared their throat. The meeting was called to order. The room grew quiet. It was filling up with cigarette smoke. The collection plate to pay for the coffee went by. I smelled my dollar before contributing. It was crisp and new. The ink tickled my nose hairs, and I sneezed. The collection plate in my hand twisted and all the coins and bills fell to the floor. I retrieved what I could. The Captain fixed on me from the podium. His stare was like an elbow in the ribs.

"Do I know you?" the Captain asked.

"It's his first time!" yelled the nine-year man from the back corner.

The Captain's eyes grew large as they do when one

glimpses a natural wonder like the aurora borealis for the first time. A hushed gasp went through the crowd. The Captain leaned forward and stood.

"It's about time you got here," he said. "And what is your name?" he asked.

I told him. They all applauded. He approached me from the podium.

"And what are you?" he continued.

"I'm a drunk," I said.

The crowd booed.

"A lush?"

"Try again," the Captain said, putting his arm around my shoulders, cradling my torso.

"Boozasaurus?"

His arm began squeezing my shoulders together. I opened my mouth but nothing came out. I was Fonzie, apologizing.

"Son, in my twenty years..." he began.

"An alcoholic?" I sputtered, leaning off to one side of the chair. Everyone applauded. The Captain returned to the podium. And so it went.

The meeting's first speaker had been sober six months.

"My name's Peter," he said, even though they all seemed to know him.

"Hi, Peter!"

"You all remember when I first came in here? I had just lost my job at the funeral home for drinking the embalming fluid, and had taken to robbing prostitutes for their cash so I could buy my booze."

"I remember!" someone shouted.

"I was hooked on porn," Peter continued. "Spent my life savings on a few months rent so I could lay in bed all day and jack off and drink myself stupid on cheap whiskey and watery beer and look at the naked women in those magazines."

I wondered if Peter had ever read any of my stuff. I could feel El Dorado calling me from Dickey's pocket. I was Gatsby pining for Daisy across the sound. I lifted myself an inch off the chair. I twisted. I crossed my legs. I clutched my chest. The Captain pointed at me.

"If you can't sit still you'll have to leave."

I sat still and clenched my teeth. El Dorado was whispering my name. Peter rambled on.

"Then I found my true calling. This group has shown me the light. Now that I'm sober I can do my life's work, and you all know what that is."

"You pound nails into your nose!" a voice in the back yelled.

"That's right," Peter concurred. "When I'm not in town I'm a traveling circus performer, a professional geek. What I've wanted to do since I was a child." He began to tear up. "I've always thought I was odd and an outcast for wanting to drive sharp metal objects into the holes in my head. The kids in school would offer to do it for me. Quite often." An air of bemused resignation fell over the crowd. "Then I discovered alcohol and didn't have to worry about being the weird one anymore. When I drank I was cool." He began sobbing. "Now…I'm not afraid."

The men erupted with applause as Peter was led away from the podium.

"Ah, what the hell do I know?" Dickey said. "I was binge drinking when I was eight. Hooked on porn? He should try being married to a nymphomaniac." He shook his head in disbelief. "I gave it to her whenever I could but it was never enough. Finally caught her sleepin' with the cable guy." He was incredulous. "That's when I got rid of her," he added.

Frank was next.

"You all know me," he began.

"Hi, Frank!" the room said sternly.

"On the Rez, growin' up, there's not much doin' 'cept watchin' tv and drinkin'. My ancestors hunted for food, for life, not for some chickenshit paleface minimum wage flipping hamburgers fifty miles away. Can't live up to the broken promises of the white man runnin' my life from across the continent..."

Frank clenched his fists. The room was silent.

"...but I found that the answer does not lie at the bottom of a tequila bottle. Now that I've crawled out of that bottle I can see better the course my action must take. That course is revolution." He grabbed the microphone. "We will not stop until justice is in place for our families and for our future generations. The revolution is coming and it WILL bring a shitrain of trouble down on anyone who stands in our way!" He slapped the microphone to the side and raised his fist in the air. "Fuck Whitey!"

Two or three people clapped lightly as Frank left the stage.

"Thank you, uh, Frank," the Captain said. "Your eloquence never shies away from the, uh, truth."

"Now there's a real man," Dickey said. "He isn't afraid to apply himself to a higher calling. He's got plans, dreams, unlike my wife. Ha, she could have at least slept with a doctor or some greasy ambulance chaser, but the cable guy? C'mon. Sounds like a letter in a porno."

He didn't even know. His wife was now a character in my next story. After I convinced Dickey to give El Dorado to me I would ask for her number.

Harry was next to speak.

"Even though I was a college professor who had written a book on particle physics and the nature of the universe my first wife still felt the need to humiliate me whenever she could."

I thought of Veronica. I sat still for this.

"The worst I can remember is when she would strap on a latex dildo and take me from behind. She would do lines of coke off my ass and put lit cigarettes out on my back if I spilled any."

The crowd collectively flinched.

"Now this sounds familiar," Dickey said. "My wife had gorgeous toes, but kissed like she was pressing a thumbtack into the wall with her tongue. She was classy, though, and vindictive as hell. Guess that's why I liked her."

Harry continued.

"My colleagues noticed that I was drinking more often, but I couldn't tell them why. Hell, I was up for the Nobel Prize. It got worse when I had an affair with my secretary."

I wanted to be able to write stories like that. I sipped my coffee and lit another cigarette with the one that was already burning.

"My secretary wouldn't humiliate me, but she was

insanely jealous. How could I have missed the signs?" Harry looked to the sky.

"You were drunk!" someone yelled.

"Yes, and I was drunk the night my secretary pulled a loaded .38 out of her bag and shot my wife in the head. At least my bartender gave me an alibi."

"Jesus," somebody muttered.

"Hey, I think I know that guy," Dickey said, slapping my arm.

"Now my secretary is on death row. Here I am. I gave up teaching physics. Now I'm a yoga instructor, clean and sober. I eat tofu three times a day, won't crush an ant, and I'm writing a self help book on mild-mannered relationships, all thanks to this program."

Harry got a standing ovation. I was the first to stand.

While we were standing four men wearing flak jackets and badges on their belts rushed in and surrounded Dickey.

"Richard 'Caviar' Dickey, you are under arrest for the murder of your wife, Beluga Tiddletwigs-Dickey," the marshal said, pushing a service revolver into Dickey's back. "If you go quietly we'll note it on the arrest report."

"Well, well, well, Marshal Marshall, I been waitin' for ya," Dickey said. "Four of ya, huh? Who dimed me?"

"Ethel the Snoozer gave you up," he said.

Dickey turned to me.

"I had to do it. Couldn't let her deceive herself any longer. Friend, my Horsemen are here. It was good to meet you. Give my therapist a ringy-ding-ding if you need to talk. He'll know what to do."

He reached in his pocket and the marshals raised their guns.

"Don't try anything sneaky, Dickey" Marshal Marshall said.

Dickey cautiously pulled out El Dorado and tossed it to me.

"That was his," he said. "He was lettin' me look at it."

"With the eyes in your pocket? Let's go, Dickey," Marshal Marshall said.

They handcuffed him, read him his rights and shoved him out. While they were cuffing Dickey his feet slid the case of rubber stamps under my chair. The legacy was passed.

I could wait no longer. I had El Dorado and was ready to jet. I made for the door but the Captain stopped me.

"Ah, ah, ah, ah," he said, his hand suddenly on my shoulder, showing me towards the podium. "Now it's your turn to share."

I looked to the exit. Frank was standing there with his arms crossed, nodding at me. I cleared my throat and spoke.

"Because of the drink," I began, "I have passed out on my front lawn, had an itinerant relationship with my girlfriend, been accused of armed robbery, done various illicit drugs..."

I stopped to register a response from the guys, but was met with a stony silence. I continued.

"...witnessed a man beaten in a wheelchair, nearly castrated my roommate's dog, been threatened with arrest by the church..."

Someone in the back coughed "Bullshit!"

"...my car was impounded, made fortune and fame as a musician, watched my French-Canadian roommate fuck a Thanksgiving turkey..."

I took a deep breath.

"...was raped for my sperm, lost my fortune, lost my job, sold a bale of drugs I found in a dumpster..."

"I don't believe this shit," someone said under their breath.

"...talked to God, seen flying rodents and laughing eyeballs, and after a night in the drunk tank I donated my blood to a reptilian cult. Now I'm sober and here. Oh," I added, "I just inherited a collection of rubber stamps."

The room was silent. I stepped back from the podium. The Captain took the microphone.

"In my twenty years of involvement with this organization I have never felt so cheap as I do right now. How horrible it is for you to barge in here and make light of these poor, helpless victims."

"That's right," a man said before he broke into sobs.

The crowd became surly.

"Yeah, fuck off!" another man said.

"You should be ashamed," the Captain concluded.

I grabbed Dickey's case and made my egress. Frank was there at the front door. He got in my face, nose to nose.

"What color is my skin?" he demanded.

I stepped back and studied his face.

"Your skin is...brown," I said.

"Yes," he said, "it is brown. You may go."

I found Dickey's therapist's name and number in the case when I got outside.

"How soon can you meet?" he said. "Do you know where the Horseneck Café is?"

I held El Dorado up in the streetlight. I was Pizarro, and Cortez was now my dog. I stashed him in my cargo trousers. Tucked off to the side in Dickey's case, concealed by the rubber stamps, was a half-finished pint of whiskey and a loaded pistol that smelled of hot gunpowder.

I turned the half-finished pint into a quarter-finished pint. I had cashed my meager severance check from the warehouse earlier in the day and had ten dollars in my pocket. The Horseneck Café was mere blocks away. Ten dollars worth of leveling the playing field.

Rap 39

JIMMY BLAKE MET ME outside the door of the Horseneck.

"Who's there?" he said.

His arms were crossed.

"Unfold yourself," he demanded. "Who comes armed through my watch, so like the king?"

I set down the case.

"Long live the king!" I said.

"Prince Hamlet, is it thou?"

"Nay, it is I, Francisco. May I pass, fair Bernardo?"

"Fuck sayeth no. 'Tis now struck twelve, get thee to bed, Francisco."

Jimmy shooed me with a waving of the top of his hand. A man in a tank top and carrying a fresh pizza came up behind me.

"Yo, where's da butt-naked ho's at?" he said, grabbing his crotch and smooching his lips. He looked around in amusement.

Jimmy opened the door for him. I stepped to follow the man through the door. Jimmy's arm came down in contention before me.

"Castle rules, good Francisco," he said. "Good night, and bid the rivals of my watch make haste."

He spoke clearly now, and was clearly employed. I picked up the case and went once around the block. I stopped out of sight. I dabbed a little of Dickey's whiskey behind each ear, in case Jimmy didn't recognize me. I went back.

"'Tis here!" he gasped. "In the same figure, like the king that's dead!"

I used his own words against him.

"How now, Bernardo! You tremble and look pale. What think you on it?" I said.

"It would be spoke to. Wouldst thou struggle?" he asked.

I looked at him.

"Thou wouldst not," I said.

"Then thou wouldst enter," he said, poking his finger into my breastbone, "but methinks you better fuckin' recognize."

I sat at the bar. It was dark and crowded and the air was filled with smoke. The people knew nothing urgent. Gnats buzzed around their heads, waiting for them to die. In a week nothing had changed.

The boy next to me at the bar must have been twelve years old. When he rested his elbows on the bar they were as high as his chin. He was wearing a pair of oversized orange shooting glasses.

"Dammit man!" he cursed.

He was nursing a Golden's beer.

"What's the problem here?" he demanded. "Whiskey and a heavy rocks glass!" The cigarette holder in his lips switched back and forth. The bartender came down the bar and poured his drink.

"Hey man," the twelve-year-old said, "is there a candy machine in this joint?"

"No," the bartender said, "no candy machine."

The man at the bar next to the kid was smoking a pipe filled with cherry tobacco.

"You need some candy?" he asked. The man spilled some tiny white-crossed pills out of a rugged prescription bottle he had pulled from his coat pocket. "Each one of these equals four hours of pure mayhem. Roll 'em up!"

The kid set a few pills on the bar, then crushed them under his thumb. He cut two lines with the edge of his notebook, then took a rolled-up matchbook cover and bent to snort it all into his nose.

"We're gonna fly away, Toto!" he yelled before he snorted.

The whole bar stopped what it was doing, and watched him snort the crushed pills like a horse on fire. Then the kid screeched like a bird, contorting his face into a long, silent scream. His shooting glasses made his young face look sinister and absurd at the same time. He was the fly that had found the ointment.

The man took the pipe from his lips.

"Hang on to the barn, Auntie Em!" he yelled.

Everyone watched him snort the other line, then they cheered.

"Hip, hip, hooray!" they shouted.

"We're goin' down with the ship!" the man yelled back.

"Hip, hip, hooray!" they shouted again.

"Electric, man, electric!" the kid added.

"Hip, hip, hooray!" they shouted a third time.

Then they went back to sucking down valuable air and getting drunk.

"That'll be five dollars," the man said to the kid.

"Fucking robbery," the kid said, sniffling and twinkling the last of the crushed pills into his nose. "Don't you know who I am?"

The kid pulled out a buckskin checkbook and wrote him a check. I had seen the man in the bar before. I thought he was an accountant because he handled more cash than the racetrack. It was clear now he was a licensed pharmacist.

Jimmy burst through the front door.

"Say, what?" he yelled. "Is that a peanut there? I have

seen nothing."

The bartender returned to us.

"See, it stalks away!" Jimmy said.

The bartender rapped the bar with his knuckles in front of me.

"Goddamn peanuts," he said. "Thinks I'm his mom."

"Haven't seen him in a while," I said.

"You didn't hear? You're lookin' at our new bouncer," the bartender said. "Got knocked out in the ring last Saturday afternoon, and when he woke up he thought he was this guy, Bernardo. Showed up here and just started guarding the door and talkin' like a college professor."

The twelve-year-old shot a look over his elbow at me.

"Ali would have squeezed that punk like a grapefruit," he said.

"You drinking?" the bartender asked.

"A Golden's sounds good," I said.

"You're lookin' at the last one," he said, pointing to the kid.

He was sucking it dry as we spoke. Then he belched and pounded the bottle on the bar.

"A cheap white wine would be nice," I said.

"I could eat some grapes and piss in a glass," the bartender said.

"That'll be fine."

El Dorado was a pocket rocket warming my femur as a stone drawn from a fire. I had regained his hand-cranked paradise faster than Milton. Now I could get back to business. The case rested under my feet. I looked around the bar for my therapist. No one fit the bill. I looked around for my angels. No one fit the wing.

The bartender topped off my wine. I sipped by leaning my lips to the glass without raising it. I made a loud slurping sound. He moved on.

The man with the cherry pipe popped it out of his mouth and ordered a double brandy. He moved around the kid with his empty snifter and sat next to me.

"Let me buy you a drink," the man offered to the bartender.

"Sorry," the bartender said, "I don't drink."

"Take my advice," the man said, pointing with his pipe. "The artifice eventually crumbles. Have a drink."

"Buy yourself one, and offer to leave a big tip," the bartender suggested, pouring a double brandy.

"I understand. I don't take my own goddamn advice. Whatever."

The bartender stared at him. The man knocked back his drink.

"Another," he said, nudging the snifter forward. "You know what my advice to myself would consist of?"

"Never end a sentence with a preposition?" the bartender said, filling his glass.

"I don't get it," the man said, dumbfounded, "I just don't get it. I see all these perfect people with their happy names and their beautiful children that are so popular. What am I? I'm ugly, that's what. People see me as a prying beast. To them I'm filled with emotional malice and hate, a monster."

He drank his brandy down in one gulp.

"I'm not a monster," he said, rapping the bar with both knuckles this time. The bartender left the bottle for him. The man turned to me.

"There's nothing wrong with you," I said.

I plucked a shot glass from the bar and reached for his bottle. His hand grabbed the neck of the bottle. We played tug of war for a moment until I released my grip. He was shaking as he set the bottle back on the counter.

"They all take advantage of me," he confided to me.

He clenched his fists in anger and swung them above his head. Then he broke down sobbing.

"I feel so goddamned incompetent," he whimpered, "impotent and invalidated. It makes me get really, really mad, like I wanna take it out on them."

He crushed the invisible them in his hands, cracking his knuckles.

"I don't know why I do it anymore. It's less than meaningless," he huffed.

"You're not meaningless," I said, reaching again for his bottle. This time he grabbed my wrist and set it gently on the bar before it even touched the brandy. He continued.

"Now I'm supposed to meet some asshole up here who

says he found my number in a suitcase at a recovery meeting. No case of mine would be at a recovery meeting, let me tell you," he said, pouring his glass full. "Something about he says I'll know what to do with it. What the fuck? I gotta solve this guy's problems? I'll tell him to buy a goddamn watch because he's fucking late!"

"You must be Doctor Tremolito."

"Mudd?" he said. "Well, well, well, our hero appears." He blew his nose into a dirty handkerchief and pointed to my nearly full wine. "You're not drinking?"

His therapy was sound. I took his advice and reached for his bottle. This time he let me pour a shot of brandy.

"Let me look at you," he said.

He cradled my cheeks in his hands and studied my face.

"Ah, yes," he began, "sexual neuroses..." he continued, "...combined with an inferiority complex..." he thoughtfully continued, "...and conflicted misanthropic delusions of grandeur."

"Check please," I said, but the bartender ignored me.

"You can overcome these flaws with your mind," Tremolito assured me, poking me in the forehead with his middle finger, "but sometimes your mind needs a little help. Take my advice. If you need to get up early in the morning set your alarm when you start drinking the night before."

"Got it," I said.

"That'll be five dollars," he said.

I gave him my last five.

"Since this is your first consultation I'll write you a prescription for free," he said. "There's a new drink on the market that will help you specifically with your problem."

He picked up a bar napkin and began writing.

"It's called La Vitale," he said. "It was invented by the U.S. Special Forces' Beverage Division." He handed the bar nap to me. "This will set you straight." He swirled his brandy and downed it. "Anything else I can help you with?"

"I need five dollars," I said.

He handed me two fives, and threw a couple more on the bar. The therapy was working. I ordered another glass of wine.

"Now, where's this case?" he asked. "Wait, that looks

familiar. That's Dickey's case."

"Dickey's done, doc. Dickey's done."

"Damn!" he said. "Damn! Damn! Damn! Double damn! We lost a good man, then."

"He just got arrested for killing his wife," I said.

"God! Damn! It!" he exclaimed.

"He left me his rubber stamp collection."

"Bet he tried to sell it to you first, right?"

"He said you would know what to do."

"Of course I would," he said. "That's *my* rubber stamp collection, he got that shit from me. I collected those things meticulously during the six months I was sober. That case is a fucking ark! As a matter of fact he sold me most of the goddamn things. Then I fell off the wagon and he bought 'em all back for the price of a pigsnort."

"Here's a refund," I said, passing the case to Tremolito.

"You keep 'em," he said, passing it back. "I've got more important things to do," he said, reaching for the brandy. "My advice would be to get another hobby. You wanna know what to do? Sell them to some chump. Stamps will kill you."

He lifted the brandy and drank directly from the bottle until it was nothing but backwash, which took about fifteen seconds. He offered the bottle to me. I accepted it.

"If you'll excuse me I have to be going," he said, easing off the stool. "If you need to reach me my number's at the bottom of the prescription."

We shook hands. He turned to depart and had to steady himself on the bar.

"Much better," he said, making his exit like a yacht.

The twelve-year-old next to us had been scribbling into his spiral notebook since he had snuffed the pills. Every once in a while he would yell out "Eeeeiiyyyeee!" and clutch at the air with his fingers. He was writing, I could tell. He screeched like a bird again, only this time a woman had snuck in and grabbed him by the earlobe.

"Little Hunter," she demanded, "just what in the hell do you think you're doing?!"

"Aw, Ma," he whined.

She tugged his ear harder, pulling him off the barstool.

"Don't you 'aw, ma' me! Your father and I have been looking all over town for you! I find you next to this?"

She pointed at me like I was an appliance.

"Ow, you swine!" he said. "Yer pinchin' my ear! I'll sue you for child endangerment!"

His litigious belligerence did nothing. She dragged him away with a heavy hand to the side of his head.

I sat for a moment. I mixed the backwash with my wine and plowed through it. Before I walked out I made my way down the hall to the bathroom. Tremolito was there, handing his business card to Little Hunter's mother.

"You gave him what?" She was incredulous. "Now he's gonna be up for a week!"

"Let me give him something to balance that out," Tremolito said.

He reached into his pocket and pulled out the same ragged prescription bottle. He pecked a few pills into his palm.

"Excuse me," I said, trying to ease my way past.

"Let me give you some advice..." he was saying.

"No," she said, "let me give *you* some advice."

I was about to tell her the advice paid in brandy, but she pressed Tremolito up against the wall. I was between him and the wall.

"Excuse..." I said, "...me."

She slapped the pills from his hand and they flew into my face, bouncing off my cheek. It was too late to open my mouth. Little Hunter immediately bent and began picking them up, shoving them in his mouth from the floor.

"Get up!" she said, pulling his shirt.

She began arguing with Tremolito, pulling him off the wall. I made my move, but after one short step she suddenly pushed Tremolito backwards into me again. The force knocked me on my heels and through the door of the ladies room. There were two women rubbing lipstick on each other. One was Veronica. She saw me in the mirror and her eyes filled with hate.

"What the fuck are you doing in here?" she screamed. "Get the fucking hell out of here!"

She threw her lipstick at my face as I turned to leave. I

turned through the stall door thinking it was the exit and locked it behind me. I was trapped. I heard lipstick and mascara tubes hitting the other side of the door. Veronica made a noise like a panther.

"I'll only be a minute," I said.

Since I was in there I faced the commode and did what I had intended. Veronica broke in with Jimmy as I was doing the shake. He busted the door open and grabbed me with the dangler still dangling.

"That's him," Veronica said, one hand on her hip, the other pointing one inch from the dangler. "That's my cock and I want it outta here." Then she flicked the glans with her finger.

Jimmy unsmilingly grabbed me by the shoulders of my shirt. He shoved me through the bar where the dangler was mocked not for its size, but for its attitude.

"The cock crew!" someone yelled.

"Shall I strike at it with my partisan?" another cried.

"Thou promised not to struggle," Jimmy said, struggling.

Then he lifted me by my belt and threw me outside.

"Methinks thou should bringst me back some peanuts," he said. "Bitch."

I sheathed the dangler and zipped. I stood outside for a minute. My second toss of the night. I was being thrown out whether I was drinking or not. It was something to consider.

The door opened. Jimmy had Tremolito by the shoulders and was throwing him out. We stood outside together for a minute. The door opened again, and Jimmy threw Dickey's case out. It bounced a couple of times on its way to us, and came open when it hit the ground. The stamps and the gun spilled out on the sidewalk at our feet.

"Well, well, well, what have we here? I'll take that," Tremolito said, shoving the gun into his pants and covering it with his shirt. "Glad I got you out of there. Mind if I crash at your place?"

I reached for my cigarettes. Left them on the bar. I turned to go back in and look for them. Veronica was there with my box of cigarettes. She stood in the doorway and emptied them on the ground, then crushed them with her foot. Then she threw the empty box at my head. I tried to avoid it, but the box curved. The corner of the box hit me pointedly above the eye and rattled away somewhere on the ground.

I collected the stamps and lifted the case.

"You never said what your advice to yourself would consist of," I said.

"Don't ask."

"I didn't."

We walked back to the house.

Rap 40

A BLOCK AWAY FROM THE HOUSE WE RAN INTO NICKY. He was hammering a poster to a telephone pole with his one-wood. He turned quick with the driver raised as we approached. Without warning Tremolito charged ahead and tackled him, wrestling the club from his hand.

"Why you wanna get up in my grill?" Nicky yelled, pulling Tremolito's head back by his hair.

They fought like plaid-skirted schoolgirls angry over a lover. I split them up and took the wood from Tremolito.

"This is my neighbor," I told him. "He plays golf."

"That explains the smooth backswing," Tremolito said, dusting himself off. "Sorry, buddy, I thought you were gonna whack us. You never can be too cautious."

I handed the driver back to Nicky. He raised it as if to strike Tremolito, then bent over in pain.

"Dude, you kicked me in my purse! I'll beat your ass if you fuck with me like that again. I'm not in the mood to be dicking around."

"Here, let me make it up to you," Tremolito said.

He pulled from his pocket a handful of items. In the dim streetlight I could make out his pipe, cherry tobacco pouch, loose change, a pack of porno playing cards and a lighter. He pecked a couple of star-crossed beauties from his prescription bottle into Nicky's demanding palm.

"This will take away the tar and hate," Tremolito said.

"Nice snack, bitch."

Tremolito thought for a second, then dashed another in his palm.

"My advice is to lay off the pills."

Nicky rattled the pills like bones for luck.

"That'll be five dollars," Tremolito said.

"What's that there?" Nicky asked, pointing at a tiny square baggie in Tremolito's hand.

"Just some eight-ball acid," Tremolito said. "How about it? You down, buddy?"

"My fucking heart's racin' just thinking about it," Nicky said. His face suddenly flushed. He wiped the fresh sweat from his upper lip. "I'll take that instead." He grabbed the baggie and threw the pills on the ground.

"I knew you were a traveler the minute I laid eyes on you. That'll be ten dollars."

"How about I just don't beat your ass right here?"

Nicky made another motion to strike with the driver, then gobbled the acid without salutation or toast.

"Now, is there a remote possibility you assholes have seen my dog?"

"Can't really say," Tremolito said. "I don't know your dog."

Nicky held up a poster in front of Tremolito's face.

"What the fuck *do* you know?" he said, twisting the club for a firm grip.

"I know I'm not looking for my dog."

Nicky threatened a third time to smite him with the club. I detoured between them to look at the poster he had nailed to the pole. It showed Tiger in a headshot. He was smiling. Under the photo was the plea.

"Missing, adorable Miniature Pinscher, spiked collar, enjoys golf, answers to whiskey and beer, last seen on way to recovery meeting tonight."

Nicky's hand was full of the posters.

"You believe this shit?" he said to me. "My fucking duffer-ass boss might have nabbed him and harvested his kidney. They'll do that shit down in T.J. Tigs just got clean, too."

"The wheel might have come off the wagon," I said.

"Find my dog!" He left us waving a whiskey-wetted

handkerchief. "Tiger! Fucking fore, dude!"

I was drunk. I had not trained in a week. Tremolito was drunk too. We were legs of the same pirate, filled with slosh and song. I thought of El Dorado in my pocket. I prayed to him for strength. While I was praying I remembered the whiskey in the case. I stopped. I pulled it out. I bogarted.

"I'm..." he mumbled, rallying hard and walking ahead, "...can't even...can't...walk down..."

He pulled through, leaving no wake.

"Lucky I'm credentialed in dispensing medication."

He stopped and turned.

"Whatcha got there?"

I handed him the whiskey. He hove and knocked the rest of it out, then swayed as if in a strong wind. He reached back and tossed the hull sideways onto someone's lawn. It was Nicky's lawn.

"I do believe I'm..." he started.

He followed the bottle face first onto the grass. He was out indeed.

I did not have the energy to drag him. Nicky would bring the hammer if I left him there. Somewhere deep in my heart I heard a church bell toll for who or what for. Deep in my heart I knew the answer. I pulled El Dorado out of my pocket. Saving the world starts with one man.

I rolled Tremolito over on his back. I held the stamp firmly in my hand. I relayed a quick shot to his forehead. Nothing happened. I lifted El Dorado higher and gave him a second demeaning shot in the same place. His eyes winced, then flickered, then opened, gazing upwards to the stars.

"I am the..." he gasped.

He came up swinging.

"Wait, what, who's that?"

He was sober and menaced by thoughts of bees or bugs.

"How did I get here?" he asked.

His hands felt the grass. He plucked a blade and held it up. Then his eyes opened fully, and he saw El Dorado for the first time. It gleamed in the streetlight. He reached out his hand to touch it, but I pulled it back. He reached out further and I pulled it back more. I turned and he reached around my body. Finally I had to put it back in my pocket.

He leaned in and hugged me. He kept hugging me. He would hug, then pull away and his eyes would be filled with tears, then he would hug me again. The streetlight reflected his entire life in his eyes.

Finally I broke free.

"Look kid," he said, "I know you're a patient and all, and, well, do you want to know a secret?"

He leaned in close.

"I can't tell you. All I can say is that I got back in the game for this job. You don't know what I've gone through to reach this place, this moment in time. It would take a thousand years to describe and we don't have a thousand years."

This I knew. I began to sway.

"I'll be blunt. I must have that stamp."

I felt something rise from deep within myself.

"I insist," he insisted.

The rising was not unlike a pint of bile, but something sweeter.

"I'll give you twenty dollars for it."

The hustle was on. I swayed in silence. I was nearing capacity.

"Playing hard to get, huh? Look, if you wanna stonewall me I should warn you you're negotiating with the best."

He dug reluctantly into his pockets.

"Make it..." he continued, counting the bills, "twenty-two..." and the change, "...fifty. I'll even throw in these porn cards."

I was nothing if not hard to get.

"Okay, I can see we've got work to do."

He looked me in the eye and studied. He pondered. He considered. He reconsidered. He considered yet again. He looked from side to side, then leaned in close.

"I am the Shepherd, boy," he whispered when he was close to my ear. Instead of tobacco and rye his breath now smelled of sassafras and lilacs.

I lifted my hand to drink, but my hand was empty. The final swig of Dickey's whiskey had put me on the ledge over the edge. I was about to go out beyond the breakers. I reached into my pants and pulled out the stamp.

"To the..." I started, then puked on Nicky's lawn. I was on my knees in the grass, clutching El Dorado.

"Let me give you some advice," Tremolito said, slapping my back.

He pulled out his prescription bottle and dappled a couple into my palm. I chewed them dry. I was on my feet quicker than Mike Tyson, sparring again with the world.

"You better let me hold the stamp for now," he suggested. "Why do you think I have the gun? We're on the same team. You think all of this shit just happens? You think you just happened to call me tonight after meeting Dickey at the meeting? No," he reasoned, "there is a reason."

"I'm on a mission from..."

"God? I may have to reconsider my diagnosis. Don't you know what that is? That stamp is Satan's only child. I'm working for God and have been sent here to guide you. We must destroy it."

"It was conceived of a great tragedy," I said.

I looked at pobre Dorado in my hand.

"You're drunk," he said, "and a narcissist, I might add."

Nicky was returning up the walk.

"You're gonna clean up that vomitus," he said. "How'd you like it if I came and puked on your grass?"

He had done just that two months before.

"You'd best not divot up my lawn." He pointed at Tremolito with the driver, then up at a pole. "I still got a couple of nails left."

"That acid hits like lightning, kid. You'll want to be off the course when it does."

Nicky flipped him off over his shoulder and continued down the walk. I was nearing my own final green. I needed to hit the clubhouse. The pills were my Mulligan. It fades after that.

The front door was locked. I reached in my pocket. My key was missing. It was late and there were no lights on. I would have to jump the fence.

"Wait here," I said.

"Okay."

I jumped over the fence. I braced for Tipsy. Nothing. I was standing there only a second when Tremolito jumped over the fence above and knocked me to the ground.

I saw a philosopher's phosphorescent flash, then awoke, dazed and dreaming. I was back at the Horseneck and everyone was nude. I had twelve Golden's in front of me, all cold. There was an endlessly absorbent bar nap under each one.

"Psst, hey Mudd!"

I looked around. It wasn't Tremolito or Nicky.

"It's me, God."

"You're in the bar nap," I said.

It was the only bar nap that was not under a beer.

"Quiet! Not so loud," he said. "I'm in-cog-nee-to."

The nap was the one on which Tremolito had written the prescription for La Vitale.

"You think I want my lady knowing I'm here working when I'm supposed to be having dinner with her? She'd wring me out like a stone. Anyway, you're here because I need a report. The angel Gabraham told me you lost your marker. What's up with that shit, fry scooper?"

"I left the stamp in a beer case."

"I told you not to lose it."

One of the beers on the bar disappeared.

"Don't pull an Adam on me, kid. You know what happened to that guy. If I find you're holdin' out on me you're gonna have an assload of troubles."

"It found its way back. Divine intervention."

"You know, Rain Man, you're funnier than a backpack of dicks," he said. "I can tell you're lying to me, barflower, but I can't figure out how. When I do you're gonna be fresh out of dicks."

"My therapist wants to hold it for me," I said. "He is working with us."

"Your therapist?"

"Doctor Tremolito."

"I also distinctly remember telling you not to show it to anybody."

Another beer disappeared.

"You stupid panty sniffer! Tremolito doesn't work for me anymore."

"He offered to buy it."

A third cold Golden's disappeared.

"He wants to buy it so that he doesn't have to take it from you. He's a thief, a liar and he's wayward as fuck. He is defunct and debunked. As a matter of fact he's so far down on my shit list I'm gonna need shoe polish to cross his name off when I'm done with him. Whatever you do, do not let him hold it."

"He's got a gun," I said.

"I don't care if he's Janie or George Fucking Steinbrenner! You need to keep that stamp away from him! I'll take care of the gun, just hold on to the stamp."

There came a call from across the bar.

"Marvin Heimlich Studebaker!"

"Alright," God said, "that's her. I'm the hell outta here. Remember, the fate of what depends on you?"

"The world."

"The world, right, the world depends on you. Don't let Trem..."

There was a flash. When I regained my bearings I realized I was on my back, and Tremolito was sitting next to me in the midnight shadow of the fence. He was holding El Dorado. I saw the morbid cupidity in his eyes. I reached up slowly with only my arm and took it back. He was hurt, relieved and avaricious in the same expression. I sat up.

"You didn't wait," I said.

"There was a maniac out there in bright orange and yellow biking shorts, comin' at me from across the lawn," he said, standing and brushing himself off.

"That was a surfboard."

"Quick board."

I turned my hand over. El Dorado caught the light and glowed before I pocketed it.

"My advice to you would be to get rid of that, that, thing as soon as you can. You've got to trust me. That stamp is all-powerful. If it falls into the wrong hands it could be used to draw forth unspeakable evil."

I opened the door to the garage.

"Look, I'm not going to beg you for the stamp."

"Okay."

He got down on his knees and clasped his hands.

"Please, please, please give me the stamp. Just let me hold it again for a second."

I shoved him into the garage. I flipped on the light. Tipsy was sleeping on my mattress. I bent and rubbed his snout.

"Does your dog bite?" Tremolito asked.

"No."

He bent to rub Tipsy's snout. Tipsy snarled and lunged at him.

"Hey!" he said. "I thought you said your dog doesn't bite?"

"That's not my dog."

"Sonofabitch ain't gonna be anybody's dog," he said, patting the gun.

"Walk this way," I said, bumping first into the doorframe.

Tremolito followed me into the darkened living room, bumping first into the doorframe. I could barely make out the couch. I pointed.

"There's your bivouac," I said.

The room stayed dark as I turned back to the garage. I heard the brutal crunch of the springs as he fell onto the couch.

At night I would hide my cigarettes from Francois under my pillow. Before I passed out I tucked El Dorado under my pillow next to the spare pack. My day of service would begin early. I would once again be righteous and sober at the same time.

Rap 41

"MUDD, WAKE UP."

It was Tremolito.

"Wake up, dammit."

He was shaking the mattress with both hands. I woke up.

"Wow," he said, "you couldn't sleep either, huh?"

"If you say so."

"Try some valerian root. Hey, I know this sounds crazy

but there's a damn dead skunk in my bed. I couldn't sleep, that couch is so lumpy, so I rolled over to get rid of the lump and felt its tiny legs."

We went to the living room to investigate.

"I'm sure he crawled in next to me while I was sleeping. Look at that crazy collar. That must have been what was jabbing me in the back."

This skunk was waxed hairless for an affluent image. It must have been an exotic local pet. Then I saw the knit beanie and shredded beer can next to the body. I looked closer at the victim.

Tiger had probably surrendered drunk in relapse before we got home. It had been at least three hours since Tremolito literally crashed on the couch. Tiger's tongue was lashing out, even in death, and his bloated body was some obscene sporting device meant to be tethered and floated in merriment above haranguing throngs.

"See what follows that stamp?" Tremolito whispered. "This is the first sign, a dead skunk is always the first sign."

"Meet Nicky's dog."

Tremolito leaned over, holding back a burp of vomit. He caught his breath and continued.

"Get rid of the body," he said. "He's starting to smell like day-old carne asada. Carpe corpus!"

There was no moon. Perfect night for a burial. The stars were too far away to testify. We had already dug a hole in the dark corner of the backyard when Tremolito had the idea to use El Dorado on Tiger. I went and got a beer from the fridge and the golden marker from under my pillow. I tried it on Tiger, but without immediate success.

"Try it again," he said.

I tried it again. Nothing.

"Try it again."

I tried it again fifteen times, and fifteen times nothing. Tiger was deader than dirt.

The dog's body made a dull thud when Tremolito dropped it into the ground. Tipsy was there and began scrambling dirt doggystyle into the hole. The wind was picking up. As we began throwing dirt a wail came from somewhere beyond the palm trees. We stopped and listened.

"What the fuck was that?" Tremolito whispered.

"That is the sound of blood boiling in fire."

"It sounded like a door. No, wait, listen, it's someone hammering." He saw an opening. "Look, I don't mean to be garrulous about that stamp."

"Okay."

"Just let me carry it. They'll be coming for you," he warned. "Hammering in the wind is the second sign. I won't let you out of my sight. They'll never suspect me. We can't let it fall into their hands."

A couple shovelfuls more and we heard a voice from over the fence.

"What's goin' on, dudes?"

It was Nicky. He jumped the fence and walked toward us. He was still carrying his one-wood.

"Here comes one of the serpents now," Tremolito said. "Don't trust him."

We began shoveling faster. Nicky got right to the point.

"Dude, that acid you gave me is bunk!"

He was flipping the driver as if Neal Cassady had chosen golf over cars or Kesey.

"No, wait, it doesn't hit you right away. It's the creeper. It's, it's..."

"It's been hours, motherfucker. Now I'm gonna pound you."

Tremolito held his ground.

"Listen, why do you think they call it 'eight-ball'? The eight-ball is the last one to pocket, right, but it wins the game? Just give it time."

Nicky was fuddled by the logic. He hesitated. He looked around.

"Whoa, you guys burying a skunk?"

He peered into the hole. Tiger's spiked collar twinkled as it caught the reflection of a shooting star.

"Wait, I don't get it. How'd the skunk get Tiger's..."

The weight of the tardy acid, the hanging of the posters, the remaining nails in his pocket, and the driver twirling in his hand combined with the tepid realization that we were pushing daisies for his dead dog.

Tremolito saw the direction Nicky was headed. He

watched the driver. He feared a fourth coming of the club, a dreaded quadruple-bogey off his childproof cap of a head. He raised his finger slowly and pointed at Tipsy.

"He did it," Tremolito said.

"What?" Nicky said. "Wait, what?"

"The little guy dug under the fence," he continued. "I caught him going through the trash, but before I could corner him that big dog there had the little bastard by the throat. They fought over a bone from a ham, and he just..."

Tremolito trailed off, searching for the words.

"He just..." he trailed off again, looking for the words in his hands.

"He just..." he trailed off a third time, looking up to Nicky.

"Just what? Just what?"

"He just...sat on him. Most of him, his head anyway. Suffocated him with those monster balls of his."

"Canine and Abel," I said.

Nicky hesitated, then raised the driver. Then he lowered it. Then he raised it again. Then he lowered it again.

"Dudes, is it time for the sun to be coming up?"

He was staring into the grave.

"Holy shit," Nicky said. "I'm looking at the fucking blazing eye of life right now."

The backyard was dark as Moses' crotch. Nicky's eyes were bulging. He was vacated like this for a few seconds, then he came home.

"Whoa, you were right about that lightning bolt, man, the trips just kicked in. Think I might stand here and talk to myself for a minute, do a little self-inventory, you know, just..."

Nicky trailed off. His lips moved, but no sound issued forth. We all stood motionless in the dark for ten minutes until Nicky picked back up.

"...so I heard the noise and, hey, what are you digging? Are you building a golf course? I super want my dog back, I miss the little guy so much, like he was my best friend, and..."

Nicky looked at Tipsy. He raised the driver.

"No, it won't make things right," Tremolito said. "Take

my advice. Just, just, just..."

"...send him away..." I whispered to Nicky.

"...send him away..." Nicky whispered to himself.

"Yes! Great idea! Just send him away," Tremolito said. "Banish him from the kingdom."

"Yes," Nicky said, "send him away." He thought for a second. "Send him far away, send him far, far away." He was on to something. "...far, far, far away, far, far, far, far..."

Nicky locked in a semantic tailspin. Tremolito turned him slowly by the shoulder as he was talking. He leaned back and nudged Nicky with his foot. Nicky moved forward. Halfway to the fence he stopped.

"Far, far away!" he said, pointing to his head, as if he had known it all along. He slapped his knee and roared like a lion. He pointed at me and mimed running, then looked far off into the distance, his hand shading his eyes from the non-existent sun. He was crying he was laughing so hard. We could hear him laughing even after he had closed his patio door behind him.

"It's not that funny," I said.

"Far, far away," Tremolito said, reaching into his pants for the gun. He pointed it at Tipsy. "Okay, fleabag, stay, you die. Move, you live. You choose."

Tipsy saw the betrayal. He was no neighborhood fool. There was nothing he could do. He was facing the wood or the lead, most likely both.

"Grrr, ruff-ruff, ruff," he said to me.

"Ruff," I said.

He turned and walked slowly toward the back gate, opening it with his nose. When the gate was cracked he turned to look back one final time. Then he walked slowly into the night.

"What did he say?"

"He said he forgives me."

I finished my beer and threw the empty bottle in the hole with Tiger's body. It either hit a rock or the dog's skull. I threw Dickey's case of stamps into the grave on top of the pile. I was done collecting. Now there was only one stamp, and it was in my grasp and in my pocket, not very far, far, far, far, far, far away.

Rap 42

AN HOUR AFTER WE BURIED TIGER I was asleep. An hour after I fell asleep I was awake again. It was just before the butt-crack of dawn, the darkest hour of the darkest day of the year. I had been dreaming of Tipsy when I heard a noise that sounded like the dog himself scratching at the garage door. I turned on the light.

There, kneeling next to my mattress with his arm stretched out and his hand under my pillow, was Doctor Tremolito. He was shrouded in the blanket from the couch, a thief in the night, his hand under my pillow and me laying there staring at him. He slowly pulled his hand out empty.

"The skunk is back," he said.

"That was a dog."

"Okay, I admit it. There is no skunk. I was going to steal the stamp. I confess!"

God was right. He was wayward as fuck, yet he continued.

"You've got to understand the latitude of what's happening here."

He pulled the gun from behind his back.

"I didn't want to have to do it this way," he said. "You leave me no other choice."

He raised the gun point blank at me.

"Will you give me the stamp?"

I was looking down the barrel.

"Very well," he said. "I consider this assisted suicide."

"See you on the cross."

I heard the click of the trigger. Then another. Then a third. This time a tiny flame popped from the top of the pistol. It was a souvenir lighter. I reached under my pillow for my cigarettes. I pulled one and lit it. I exhaled and a clap of lightningless thunder broke outside the window.

Tremolito was defeated. He dropped the blanket from his shoulders. I saw it in his eyes. He looked down, then looked up at me in sadness. The sadness gave way to gratitude and then contempt, followed by resignation.

Then he began to recoil. He recoiled in horror. He

recoiled in frozen panic. He recoiled in wincing love. He recoiled in-a-gadda-davida, baby. He was petrified. He opened his mouth to scream, but produced only a minor chirp from his pill-inflected larynx. He pointed behind me.

"It's back," he whispered. "It's..."

I sat up and turned. I recoiled. A glowingly transparent Tiger jumped up on the mattress to my side. He was dragging a gnarled and translucent beer can at the end of his invisible leash. The ghost snarled at Tremolito, snapping the oxygen from the air. Tremolito reached out to throttle the spirit but his hands could find no grip. Tiger leapt and dogpaddled through the air until he faded through the wall. Then there was silence. Tremolito and I looked at each other.

"Spirit visitation is the third and final sign," he said.

My response was cut off by a noise from the corner. Something was moving in the dark under the utility sink. We looked at each other, then we looked at the dark under the utility sink. A mass of black pelt the size of a large cleat brush with a white stripe down its back waddled from the dark and yawned.

"Now that's a skunk," I said.

We meant to move in two directions at once. Instead we ran into each other. The skunk's tail was pre-spray tight, and he looked chafed as he approached. We were cornered in a dead-end game, sure to stink for weeks. The skunk stopped and opened his pointed mouth.

"Doc, I need to see you in my office."

Tremolito shuffled backwards on his knees, his arms outstretched for balance, never taking his eyes off the skunk. The skunk took a step forward.

"I can have you making toys at the North Pole with Santa by sunrise!"

Tremolito's back was up against a shelf filled with car parts.

"Not that you'll see the sun up there for another three fucking months."

Tremolito's crinkled fingers danced in confusion in front of his face. The skunk took another step forward.

"It's Christmas every day of the year up there, bitch-ass."

"No! Anything but that!"

Then another voice, father away.

"Marvin, come back to bed!"

Tremolito stood in sudden empowerment at the unexpected diversion. As he stood he let loose a moist cry of flatulence in his pants. He shook his fist at the skunk.

"See *this* in your office!" Tremolito slapped his arm and showed the skunk his derogatory elbow. "You haven't heard the last of me, big man!"

He pulled the blanket back over his head with a stiff-arm matador move and retreated to the couch, his eyes never leaving the skunk. The air of his fart lingered over my bed like a sour apple ready to fall from the tree.

"See what I mean?" the skunk said. "A leopard don't change his spots."

"Marvin!"

The skunk exploded in a cloud of black smoke. The smell of singed skunk hair combined with Tremolito's gas to carouse in my dreams when I finally fell asleep at sunrise.

Rap 43

TIGER'S GHOST REAPPEARED IN CHAINS of beer cans the next night. The second night he came headless and barking out of his anus. The third night he came shrouded as some faceless infinity under a cloak of young goat's hair. The fourth night Tremolito called a dog exorcist.

The nights were long. I would dream of Tiger's ghost roaming the neighborhood. Tiny claws would scratch at the garage door, but nothing was there. I would find beer cans, empty and shredded, that no one had finished. I dreamed of a ghastly Tiger, headless and floating, dog paddling through the air above my mattress. I inspected the grave each day, but it had not been disturbed.

Tipsy had fled into exile, a hunted dog, fated to wander the earth for a crime of passion he did not commit. Nothing left but to work and run. Neighborhood cats went missing. The house was on edge, ready for anything. Anything except Francois.

Francois had discovered my sixpack of La Vitale before I could try it. He told me he thought I had stashed some kind of exotic alcohol. He finished half a bottle and invested in a set of free weights for the front lawn. When the bottle had a few sips left he enrolled in a kickboxing school downtown. By the time the bottle was routed he had spoken of becoming a cowboy and bemoaned us as couch sissies.

"Why you are afraid ze ghost ze silly dog, Mudds?"

He handed me a bottle of La Vitale. After one sip I had given up smoking and was running ten miles a day. When my first bottle was finished I went to the mountains for a day looking for cougars to wrestle. I pinned two and bit their testicles before kicking them down the hillside.

Francois went along to a logging camp to cut timber and took the remaining four bottles. He ended up staying overnight to help fight a wildfire. The trumpet of the wild was sounding from long ago and far away.

The stores were sold out of La Vitale. Cowardice soon followed. My stash of cigarettes in the freezer was gone, one pack left. I had to hock my typewriter for food. Any manuscripts were written longhand by the stub of a pencil sharpened with a rusty razor blade. I sold my blood for beer money. I still owed the judge five-hundred and my thirty days were almost up. My coach was now a tobacco-colored pumpkin.

I came home the day after Christmas. The sun in his merry sky had dried up for the day and a winter cold front had moved in. I was returning to the house from Miguel's truck with a dime bag purchased with a dime of blood money. Before I could close the door a voice called from where it was crouched in the darkness behind the couch.

"She's here."

It was Tremolito. I turned on the lights. Tremolito was pointing discreetly at a woman in black slacks, white shirt and skinny black tie. Next to the woman was a tony and stark white German Shepherd wearing an identical skinny black tie around his neck. Next to the Shepherd was the couch, and behind the couch was Tremolito pointing discreetly at the woman. There was a quiver of pina colada incense burning.

"I'm glad you could come out on such short notice, Jo," Tremolito was saying.

"Please come out from behind the couch, sir."

"But the wolf..."

"He's had his shots."

"As I was saying," he said, standing and looking around the room, "spirit abatement is not exactly an easy skill set to find in the phonebook."

"I'm not Joe," she said, "he's Joe."

"Who's Joe?"

"Him."

"Who him?"

"Him," she said again, banking her head down at the Shepherd.

Joe sat at attention, his keen eyes scanning the room for ghosts.

"I guess I thought..."

"Thought what?"

"Thought that..."

"Thought that what?"

"I thought..."

"You did call for a dog exorcist, did you not?"

"I did, but..."

"But what?"

Tremolito had no advice for her but what.

"That's what I thought," she said. "I'm Peachy, and yes, Holy Joe is half-wolf."

"Joe is..." Tremolito considered, looking at her. "This is difficult for me to say." He turned to me and explained. "Joe is going to get rid of Tiger's ghost for us."

He produced one of Tiger's "Missing" posters. Holy Joe proficiently sniffed it, then got to work. He moved around behind us. He stuffed his adroit nose in our bungs, sniffing each hole with the alacrity of Edison studying filament.

"He has to do this to insure the spirit has not taken hold in a member of the household," Peachy said.

When Joe reached Tremolito his ears became pointed and he began barking viciously at his asshole.

"What the hell?" Tremolito said.

"He doesn't like assholes," she said.

"Then why does his have to stick his nose all up in them?"

"I don't think that's what she meant," I said.

"Purity is key before the process can begin. What's up, Joe?"

Joe stopped barking and gave a couple of low growls to Peachy.

"Joe doesn't like you," she said to Tremolito. "He says you are somehow impure, but for now he can work around it. Now, let's all join hands and paws in a circle."

We formed the séance. Joe immediately stiffened and began to bark in tongues.

"He's speaking to Tiger now," Peachy said.

"Awwrrr, ruff, grrr," Joe said.

"Tiger is telling him that he was tried in a court of dog limbo by a jury of cats, and sentenced to an eternity of anger and toy mice."

"Barrrrrroowww, ruff, ruff."

"Tiger says he wants to come home."

"Grrrr, grrrr, ruff, awrrow."

"Tiger says it's dark where he is and he can't see."

"Rufffff, grrrr, grrrr."

"He says he will be a good dog, and that he's sorry for all the pain he has caused people."

"Repent!" Tremolito screamed.

"Ruff, ruff."

"What?" Peachy asked.

"Ruff, grrrrr, wrooow."

"The spirit is taunting him now."

Joe barked.

"Ruff, ruff!"

"He says, 'Devil dog, get out of this house!'"

Joe barked again.

"He says it again, 'Devil dog get out of this man's house!'"

Joe hesitated, cooling his muzzle, then perked his ears. He was listening to an echo in a chamber that only dogs may enter. He took off running through the house.

"He's chasing the spirit," Peachy said, running after him.

I could hear Joe barking in one of the bedrooms. Closet

doors were opened and slammed shut. The same with drawers. They were tearing up the back rooms. I looked at Tremolito. He shrugged.

"He's an exorcist, what can I say?"

While Joe was hard at work Jack came home. He saw Peachy in the kitchen opening and closing the cupboards. Joe would scratch at another, and she would open it for examination.

"Who's that?" Jack said.

"That's just Peachy," I said, "and Holy Joe. Her dog. The exorcist."

"Her dog the whatorcist?"

"That's what I said."

"You're saying that dog there will be able to get rid of the little Tiger-shit's ghost? What about Nicky? He's a dog catcher, and it's his dog anyway."

Joe saw Jack and ran back into the living room, his claws clacking on the hardwood floor. He sniffed Jack's ass, then looked up at Peachy and barked.

"He says you've suffered a great loss."

"My dog sat on your ghost. I haven't seen him since. You might say I'm a little upset."

Joe's ears perked and he began barking.

"He says..." Peachy translated, listening now with concern.

"Awwwrrrr..."

"...in order to..."

"...grrrggrrrr..."

"...finish the job..."

"...ruff-ruff, awwrrr..."

"...he needs..."

"...ruff-ruff-ruff."

"You need what?" she asked.

"Ruff-ruff-ruff," he insisted.

"He says in order to finish the job he needs..."

Joe barked twice then rolled over.

"He needs biscuits."

The room let out a cry of air.

"We're fresh out," Jack said.

"Grrrrr, ruff."

"Peanut butter flavored biscuits."

"Tipsy never liked biscuits. He preferred flesh."

"Is there any way he could do it with a cracker?" Tremolito suggested.

"No, it has to be biscuits," Peachy said. "Peanut butter flavor, Happy Dog Brand."

"I've seen those at Manny's," I said.

"Looks like we're going to Manny's," Tremolito said.

"Grrr, ruff, ruff, grrrr."

"He doesn't want you to go," Peachy said to Tremolito. "Only him."

She pointed at me.

"I think I'll stay here," he said.

They marched me out the door.

"Does Manny have beer to go with those biscuits?" Peachy asked.

The magic question. I headed towards Manny's. He was the only one open. Families were gathered behind closed doors and holiday lights. Peace on Earth, goodwill to man.

"Just remember to stay focused," Peachy whispered. "Once the exorcism is started it must be completed with haste. To leave it unfinished would be unacceptable. Just remember, biscuits, biscuits, biscuits..."

"Biscuits, biscuits, crackers..." I said.

"No, like this: Biscuits, biscuits, biscuits..."

"Biscuits, crackers, crack...biscuits..."

"Woof, grrrrr, bow-wow."

"Joe says the spirit may have, in some way, compromised your ability to communicate. Just do as I say."

Manny would eat us alive.

We were approaching a bus stop. A streetlight flickered on and off, and the wind blew out of the North. A man was seated on the bench. He saw us coming and stood up.

"Hey," he said as a humble smile spread across his face, "I'll trade you a joint for bus fare."

He showed us a fat bone. I reached out but Peachy smacked it down.

"I've gotta get to the VA before they close," he said. "There's only one more bus tonight." He was dirty and shivered in the damp wind. He had no shoes and his toenails were extravagantly long and muddy. "It's only a buck, and this stuff is good."

Peachy pushed past me.

"Yeah," she said, "well I'm a cop and I'm gonna have to confiscate this contraband as evidence."

Peachy plucked the jay from between the man's fingers, and pushed him backwards over the bench into the street. She confidently broke the bone in two, and flecked the contents into the gutter. The man stood up slowly.

"Aw, bummer, man," he said. "Why are you such a bully? It's the day after Christmas."

"Just consider this your gift receipt," Peachy said.

He held out an open hand to me. "I got nowhere to go." He grabbed my arm. "If you're cops you should help me."

"Yeah," Peachy said with a snort, "here's my badge."

Peachy reached back and punched the man in the face. Joe flew into a holy rage, his snapping teeth inches from the man's jugular. He was his own squadron, an authority gone wrong. Blood flew from the man's nose and eyes. He fell back over the bench again. This time Peachy followed him.

"Hey, man," the man begged, crawling backwards into the street, "I didn't do nothin'."

"Shut up, asshole," Peachy hissed. "You were askin' for it when you took possession of that marijuana cigarette!"

Peachy set upon the man like a Keith Moon solo. Joe was the ultimate right-hand-man, an intimidator, raining the kill-barks on him as he was beaten in the gutter. A family across the street watched from their front room, then closed the curtains. Peachy beat the man savagely, then went through his pockets as he lay moaning on the ground.

"See," Peachy said, standing up, "motherfucker was lying to us. Never trust a pot smoker."

She held up a couple of crumpled and dirty dollar bills in the streetlight.

"Aawwwrrrr, grrr, grrr, ruff."

"Joe says a couple more like him and we don't have to pay for shit."

Peachy kicked the man in his head. He was spitting and rolling in the street, breathing for mercy.

"Don't quit," the man implored. "It's so quiet. Help me..."

"You're fine. Stop acting," Peachy said, pushing me ahead down the sidewalk. "Let's go get us some beers. Remember, do as I say, and we'll have that ghost terminated with prejudice as soon as we get back."

Manny was about to lock his front door when we arrived.

"Not so fast," Peachy said, pushing Manny through the door.

We all went in and Peachy locked the door behind us. Manny went for his gun under the counter. Joe was on it. He backed Manny up against the cigarette case. Peachy grabbed his gun.

"Rufff, grrrr, grrrrr, awrrr, grrr."

"Joe says don't just stand there, go get the Happy Dogs. Me and Manny are gonna go find his safe. Don't forget the beers."

Peachy and Joe led Manny to the back room. I went for the beer and the biscuits. My moment alone was a revelation. I opened the Happy Dog box and tried one. Crispy and meaty, with a nice peanut butter bouquet.

"Alright, gentlemen," Peachy said, "let's get the fuck outta here. You got the biscuits?"

I rattled the box as evidence. Joe had grabbed the keys to Manny's car from his belt. It was parked out front. I could hear Manny yelling from the back room as we loaded the beer in the back.

"I cut your balls off when I get you. You no steal from Manny. I kill you!"

The car was huge and drove like a wet burrito. Peachy laughed, gassing it and flipping the top off a beer at the same time. She was crazed with beer and power, shooting out stoplights as we roared past. She eased up as we turned down my block.

"Let's put it in the garage," Peachy said.

"It's full," I said. "That's where I sleep."

"You live in the fuckin' garage?" Peachy said, spitting beer on the windshield.

"Grrrr, ruff, ruff."

"Joe says you're a fuckin' loser," she added.

"Park in Nicky's driveway," I suggested.

Joe nodded. They both agreed it was a sound idea.

Back in the house Joe arranged the biscuits in a peanut butter-flavored pentagram on the floor. The pentagram was open at one point, and a short trail led into the empty and waiting Happy Dog box.

"He's baiting the spirit," Peachy whispered.

We watched as the biscuits disappeared one at a time. There was the sound of invisible crunching.

"Grrr, awwrooo, ruff, ruff."

"Joe says no one can resist a Happy Dog."

I did not argue. Tiger was following the trail into the empty box. When he was inside Peachy tipped it up and closed the lid. The box began shaking as the spirit tried to escape.

"That's it," Peachy said. "Now you can do what you want with him."

"Rufff, bark-bark, grrr ruff."

"Joe says that will be five-hundred for the service, and thank you for the biscuits."

"Ruff, grrrr."

"No checks, please."

"I thought you said one-hundred to rid the house and property of a Miniature Pinscher?" Tremolito asked.

"Ruff-ruff, grrr."

"One-hundred is the base fee."

"Arrrww, grrr, ruff."

"He says while he was speaking to Tiger the spirit revealed to him the true circumstances surrounding his death. For an extra four-hundred Joe will tell you how the deceased met their demise. Joe?"

"Ahh, no thank you," Tremolito said. "We'll pass."

"Tipsy sat on him, right?" Jack said.

Tremolito urged them out the door.

"Guess you gotta be on your way, right?"

Holy Joe put his paws on Peachy's shoulders and whispered in her ear.

"Grrrrrr."

"That's what you were told, but it appears the circumstances were more duplicitous. We feel this is information you would like to know."

Peachy was staring at Tremolito.

"How is Joe certain of this stuff?" Jack asked.

"Don't know. He's just crazy like that."

"Awwrrr, grrrr, bark, ruff."

"He says if there were no foul play involved the spirit would not be haunting the house."

"Grrr, grrrr, ruff, ruff."

"What if I don't want to pay the extra?" Tremolito posited.

He lifted his shirt to reveal the gun in his belt.

"How about we just keep it at one-hundred," he said.

"Then I guess we gotta take this to the proper authorities."

"They'll never believe you, just because he's wearing a tie. He's a dog."

"Five-hundred is the bill. Consider the extra four a bullshit tax. You are now a licensed chef of shit. As a matter of fact, since you are taking up so much time, and had no dog biscuits ready as stated in our verbal contract, why don't we make it an even thousand."

Peachy opened her vest to reveal Manny's much larger gun.

"I'll take that," she said, pulling the gun from Tremolito's belt. "Now, why don't you just give me the thousand."

"Are you shitting me?" Tremolito asked.

"Would I shit you? You're my new favorite turd. The bill is a thousand, or we find out what really happened to the dearly departed."

Joe stood up, growling and advancing at Tremolito.

"Okay, take it easy," Tremolito said. "Like I said, let's make it five-hundred."

Joe's growl grew louder.

"Okay, fine, six."

"Rufff, grrrrr!"

"Okay, a thousand. Just make sure that damn ghost is gone."

Tremolito pulled out a minor gangsta roll. He snapped off the rubber band, and counted out fifties and hundreds.

"What if I want to know what happened?" Jack asked.

"That's another thousand."

"Well, shit, I'm about a thousand short there," Jack said.

"Hey dude, what about the couch rent you owe me for the last week?"

"It's only been a few days."

Tremolito handed Jack a hundred.

"Prorate that shit," he said.

Peachy reached out and grabbed the roll from Tremolito and the hundred from Jack.

"No need to count the rest," she said. "I trust you."

"This is robbery," Tremolito said.

"No," she pointed out, "just business as usual. Okay, buddy, what you got on you?"

She pointed the gun at me. I had been carrying El Dorado with me while Tremolito was crashing on the couch. I stood silent, and Peachy patted me down. She hit on the stamp.

"Is that a Happy Dog in your pocket or are you just glad to see me?"

Peachy held up the stamp.

"What's this, some sort of tribal butt-plug fetish?"

"I wouldn't do that if I were you," Tremolito said.

She buried the stamp with the cash in her pocket.

"We'll be leaving now," she said.

There was a silence, as if we all knew something was about to happen. Then the screen door opened. Someone was arriving. The front doorknob turned. Everyone waited. The door opened slowly, and Francois stepped into the room.

He was wearing a lumberjack's flannel and a burly turtleneck under a thick, fringed-leather coat. He carried what must have been a hundred pound rucksack on his back.

"You're home early," I said.

"Oui," he said, setting the bag down and taking off his coat. "Ze fire we extinguish. I must save twenty men from ze circle of flame. We almost-ed to die."

His voice had grown deep since La Vitale. His face was seared with smoke and vim, darker than a vigorous bourguignon.

"Who's this?" Peachy demanded.

"This," I said, "is Francois."

"You sound like a gor-met," Peachy said, as if speaking

of a ballet, aiming Manny's gun at his chest.

"Perhaps, yez, one day I go to ze culinary zchool."

Francois' eyes lit with a hidden meanness, a primal wood-chopping strength I had never seen before. He was choosing his words carefully. He confidently removed first his flannel, then his turtleneck to reveal a frame that had bulked up by forty pounds in only a few days. In his wife-beater he was ripped. He moved calmly in front of Peachy and Joe.

"Why do you ask me zis question?" Francois said, raising one eyebrow.

"Because I think you should hand over that bag," Peachy said. "Then make me a fish taco, punk."

Francois' expression shifted to the other side of his face.

"Fizsh taco?" he whispered. "Punks?"

The room was tense. No one spoke. In the standoff I saw out the window behind Peachy a floating steamroller bong. The bowl was lit, but instead of rising into the tube smoke began to rise from Peachy's pants. Ethos and pathos were about to meet. El Dorado was stepping in.

There was a flash, and Peachy's pants exploded from her body. With no pants El Dorado fell to the floor, now white hot and glowing. Before she could raise the gun Francois slapped it from her hand like an unfiltered cigarette from a child. The gun flew across the room. It discharged when it hit the far wall, striking Francois in the buttocks. He winced like a man when bitten by an ant.

"Iz no good," he said.

He then proceeded to grab Peachy by her skinny black tie, and pummel her about the face. It all happened so fast Peachy never had a chance. Joe made for the gun, but Francois chucked Peachy's bottle of beer like a tomahawk and caught him on the back of the head. He continued to imbue Peachy with body blows until she was limp. In a flash he ripped the laces from his combat boots and hogtied her.

Jack called the police. Before they arrived I went through Peachy's pockets and pulled out Tremolito's roll, plus an extra five hundreds and a ten dollar bill. Enough for the judge and a bottle of wine. I stuffed the hundreds in my pocket, and returned the roll to Tremolito. El Dorado was still too hot to handle.

The squad cars pulled up in front of Nicky's house and surrounded Manny's car. They broke down Nicky's front door, and in less than five seconds were pulling him out on the lawn to be processed in his underwear while wearing a bag of golf clubs over his shoulder.

"Wrong house!" Jack yelled.

They left Nicky cuffed on his lawn. As soon as they saw Tremolito they had him down on the floor.

"Wrong man!" Jack yelled.

They turned and threw Jack to the floor, ready with the cuffs.

"It's her and the dog," I said.

In the confusion I saw Tremolito reaching across the floor. His fingers were aching for El Dorado. His arm was shaking it was stretched so far. Finally his fingertips touched the golden prize.

The police had Peachy cuffed and Joe muzzled.

"What kind of a dipshit tries a shakedown with a novelty lighter?" I heard one of them sneer.

They laughed and led the perps out the door. I thought of the lighter and looked again at Tremolito, but he was gone. I thought of Peachy's gun. That was gone too. I thought of El Dorado. He was gone three.

I walked outside. El Dorado was Christopher Cross, and Tremolito was the wind, his figure cutting a silhouette of desperation as he ran up the street, barking from his haunted ass all the way.

I grabbed a couple of Peachy's beers and walked over to Nicky's lawn. I handed Nicky a beer as he sat in his underwear, leaning on his bag of clubs.

"You won't believe it, dude. Since your buddy gave me those creeper trips I broke par for the first time," he said, twisting the top off.

"Might want to send a thank-you card."

"My boss hasn't beaten me since before Thanksgiving. Now I'm a full time muthafuckin' dog catcher, dogg! I'm playing with the mayor next week."

"You'll be pro in no time," I said.

I still had the dime bag of weed in my pocket. Francois

refused to go to the hospital. He had removed the bullet from his buttock using a mirror, a pair of needle-nose pliers, and a fifth of whiskey he pulled out of his bag to sterilize the wound. Nicky put on some pants and we went inside to get stoned.

"Lafayette, you are here!" Nicky shouted.

"My name," Francois said, pulling Nicky around to meet his eyes, "is Francois."

Francois indeed.

Rap 44

STILL I DREAMED OF TIGER. His luminescent figure would drag chewed-up beer cans down a neatly trimmed fairway, chasing phantom golf balls. Then he would chase Tremolito's balls. Then he would chase his own balls. Then he chased my balls down the fairway. He cornered me in a high sand trap. I woke up sweating. I lit a cigarette. I looked at the Happy Dog box on the shelf.

The money from Peachy's pocket paid off the judge. I had no job and no writing work. The stores had restocked their supply of La Vitale, but I was broke. Veronica hadn't called. This time we were through for good. I saw only reflection and calculation. Once again I was a sunspot in my own solar system.

Tremolito had escaped with El Dorado. Each place I dogged him I was sent further on. He was always just out of my reach. I would find only evidence. Each new clue added another piece to an ever-expanding puzzle. God was all up in my shit to reclaim the holy stamp.

I sobered up for the quest. Francois shared with me his last bottle of La Vitale.

"You have earn-ed it, Mudds," he said to me between reps of bench presses as I was spotting for him on the front lawn.

I placed an ad for a crusade posse. I received only two responses. One was from Dickey, writing from prison.

"Love to join you pal, but, well, times are hard."

The other was Kid Basker. His nose was pierced and his shorts were baggy. They betrayed his boxers by hanging low. He kept pulling them up and waddled as he walked. Tremolito had baited him with advice before scamming him out of five dollars. Then he had pushed him to the ground and pinched his custom deck from under his feet.

"Right in front of my fucking mom's house!"

I grabbed a spare BMX bike from the garage. Basker jumped on the pegs. I pedaled.

We chased Tremolito across town, where he physically ran into a funeral full of bearers and spilled the casket. The bearers attacked us, and in the confusion he jumped on a motorcycle and took off. The crowd of bearers chased him. Basker and I looked down. Tremolito's prescription bottle lay on the sidewalk in front of the funeral home. It was empty.

The bearers were a bike gang in leather called the Swine Flu Bike Club. Tremolito had escaped their pursuit. The chapter president was named Fitch. It was his bike Tremolito had taken.

"We are going to delay his pleasure with process," Fitch promised.

A couple of them were slapping socket wrenches into their palms.

"In Illinois," he said, "I used to race coal trains for hundreds of miles, Mr. Davis. That's why I'm so good. I got endurance. We'll get his ass."

"Mudd."

"What's that?"

"My name."

"That's cool, Mr. Davis, whatever you say. We're dealin' with the Devil here, and losin' comes easy. I ain't up for losin'."

Basker and I joined forces with the Swine to chase Tremolito east across the desert. The club loaned us a chopper. I picked the bugs out of my teeth with a jackknife at eighty-five mph. My face became raw with the dust of chance, of fate. We would stop and pace up and down in front of the sunset, smoking cigarettes. Destiny blinded us but we rode on.

We chased him to the Grand Canyon, where even in winter there were four-score and seven-thousand people with cameras baiting nature's grandest ass-crack. They were weeping, supplicating, humping rocks, chasing each other and necking as they looked out over the abyss. A graying man in plaid pants, socks and sandals was videotaping it all.

"Times Square was better than this shit," he said to his wife.

A light wind of grandeur picked up and dropped down into the chasm as the air cooled. It blew up one leg of my shorts and down the other. I reached for the cigarette behind my ear and noticed some dandruff on my shoulder. I brushed it off.

We camped that evening in the pines near the rim. We sat around the campfire telling ghost stories. I told them about Tiger, and the gruesome events that led to his stayed heavenly admission.

"Aw, that ain't nuthin' to be afraid of, Mr. Davis," Fitch said.

"Mudd."

"I just wonder what we're gonna eat in heaven."

"Creamed corn," I said. "From a can."

"I'll be eating baked beans," Basker said. "From a can."

"You can have both beans and corn in heaven," a voice said.

"Wait, who said that?"

"It is I, the angel Gabraham."

"Gabrawhothefuck?"

"You may call me Gabe."

A figure sporting satin robes and a nasty set of chrome wings materialized from the piney dusk.

"What did you expect," he said, "a burning bong?"

God could only send Gabraham as backup.

"Tremolito used to be a student of mine. In time he became my partner. Then he began to lose focus. He started collecting those, those, those, those..."

He could barely utter the words.

"...those, those, those damnable rubber stamps! Damn those stamps, damn, damn them!"

He paused to reflect.

"Let's go," he said. "We have work to do."

We all banged our cans of tuna together in a toast.

"Hey look," Fitch said, standing and pointing skyward with his socket wrench, "a shooting star."

Just after sundown the full moon began to rise. The darkened sienna landscape turned a cool blue. We made our way through the pines. I could smell patchouli and sage in the distance. I saw a fire through the trees.

We hid behind some rocks. In the periphery of light from the fire there were half-naked people donned with animal skins and feathers dancing around the flames. Their faces were painted with a color that gave off an odd hue in the firelight. Their hair was unwashed and thatchy. They passed pipes that burned with magic, and were carved from what appeared to be hollowed-out cactus arms. They would inhale and bark like a parcel of perfidious and perditious seals.

"This is the Grand Canyon Man Festival," Gabraham said. "They will be branding and burning Tremolito as a symbol of renewal. Takes place on the first full moon following each Millennium. What you are witnessing is a unique spectacle. If we are caught we will most likely be branded for life or burned alive. Well, not me, but you will. They may look like hippies, but they are savages. Exercise caution. Do not get busted."

The barks were rising, then suddenly stopped. The people carried from the darkness a man on a spit. It was Tremolito, and for the first time since knowing him he was not talking. His arm was raised and I could see El Dorado clutched in his hand, ready to stamp.

"Watch how the stamp drives him mad," Gabraham tutored. "First he hates the stamp..."

Tremolito strangled El Dorado, swinging it from side to side, then made to throw it, stopping at the last instant.

"...then he loves the stamp..."

Tremolito hugged and kissed El Dorado, holding it to his breast and whispering sweet nothings to it.

"...then he wants to twist it like a pepper grinder."

Tremolito twisted it like a pepper grinder.

"He is fate intertwined with the human condition, ground into seasoning for your canned goods."

"Wow, that's really pretty, what you said just now," Basker said.

"Thank you."

A woman in lambswool headgear threw her rams-hide cape open and bent over. The tallest man pulled a branding iron from the fire. He held it red and glowing above the crowd, then remanded the burning end to the woman's bare ass. I could hear the cooking flesh hiss and pop. When the iron was removed it left a seething red can opener on her butt cheek. The crowd winced in their merriment.

"Oooh..." they muttered.

Everyone got branded with the almighty iron there on the precipice of the Grand Canyon while we watched. Tremolito was the only one left. He lifted El Dorado high. The crowd silenced.

"Stand by, men," Gabraham said. "He stirs."

The tall man turned at Gabraham's words.

"Stand by, men. We've been seen."

Tremolito saw us as well. He called out to the shadows beyond the fire from the sacrificial rod.

"I have to die with it in my hand. You don't understand!"

"Stand by, men. He explains himself."

"He speaks to me," I said.

"I'll take you down with me! We'll all burn in the flames of hell!"

We turned to flee but were surrounded by hirsute thugs wielding manual cattle prods. Our captors led us to the circle around the fire and forced us to our knees.

The tall man ran over and slapped Tremolito and poked him in the eyes, then motioned for the others. They lifted his stake from the ground and carried it to the light of the fire. They turned him over so he was facing the ground. It took two of them to get his pants down.

The branding iron was pulled from the fire. We watched as it was pressed to his skin. When it was removed there was no brand to be seen. The crowd began muttering. The tall man tried the other cheek. The iron was pressed again to his flesh, but no brand would hold. It was as if Tremolito was made of rock. He could not be branded.

"False prophet!" the tall man yelled.

The people started barking.

"Brand me you fools! You have to do this for me!" Tremolito screamed. "I have the stamp!"

"For your transgression," the tall man said, "you will be stoned!"

"Sounds fine to me," Fitch said. "I got a lighter."

They untied Tremolito and kicked him to the edge of the fire. The crowd picked up handfuls of rocks and pebbles and hurled them at him. He drew Peachy's gun, but realized he was outnumbered. In his hesitation a stone rapped his forehead.

"Shit, that hurts!"

He backed into the darkness.

"I still have the stamp!"

Another stone found his nose. He turned to run. He feinted. He dodged. He undulated. He gamboled to avoid the stones, but somehow they all found their mark. He was quickly swallowed by the high desert night.

Our posse stood in the distraction and moved to chase him. The stoners blocked our escape. The tall man spoke.

"Who among you would take his place?"

No one moved. An eyebrow was raised. Glances were exchanged. In the tense moment I felt a socket wrench in my kidney and jumped forward. The tall man put his hand on my shoulder. I assumed Tremolito's condition at the stake.

They tied me to the rod and branded me with the can opener by the light of the fire. The people in animal skins surrounded us in amazement. My brand bled gold instead of purple. The cabal bowed down as I was lifted and carried to the fire.

This was it. I was to be the millennial sacrifice. The fire nipped and roared at my head. Hairs began to fizzle and burn. The last thing I smelled was patchouli. Then someone from the rear of the crowd yelled.

"Hey! That guy took my pipe!"

Everyone stopped, and after a brief silence there was a great shout. My conveyors dropped me and ran after Tremolito into the darkness.

Rap 45

WE CHASED HIM TO SAN FRANCISCO, joined by the festive cadre from the fire. They sought to capture and idolize Tremolito as solace for the pipe he had taken. They were not the only ones.

We were joined by Midge Middlefoot, a lanky tri-athlete looking for the racing bike Tremolito had knocked her from on the road west of Flagstaff. Then there was Farley Fleetman, the winded endurance runner whose shoes had been pulled from his stinky feet by Tremolito between Death Valley and Vegas. Farley was followed by the rodeo clown Mosey Bales, who lost his barrel when Tremolito used it to roll down the Western Sierra above Visalia as we closed in on him once again. In between there was Hy Stonedrop and Cliff Hangbanger the professional rock-climbing team, Eternity Summers the snowboarder, Henna Winters the surfer, Dirk Allthumb the disc-golfer, and Mary Smith, a soccer-mom in a rented minivan, all enjoined in the quest to regain that which had been stripped from them.

Supporting this battalion of revenge was an even larger army of road cooks in roach coaches, leather craftsmen in tie-dye minibuses, sharpshooters and shiv-men, shoe-techs, trackers and shoe-tech trackers, masseurs, promoters, mechanics, cleaning ladies, mechanics cleaning ladies, ladies cleaning mechanics, organic Quaker bakers, and apprentices in the ways of whipping someone with a tire chain. I adhered a pack of cigarettes to my handlebars and nominated my conditions from a stone outcropping above the crowd.

"If any of ye captures him, and brings home El Dorado, the pack is his."

I paused.

"If I capture him, there will be a pack for each of ye."

I paused again.

"Go now."

As we found the Golden Gate Bridge the fog parted and rolled out to sea. We paused beneath the long, hard, cold steel that stood straight as it rose from the waters of the bay.

"Mr. Davis, look, up on the rail!"

It was Tremolito. We cornered him on the bridge. He had a rope around his neck. In one hand he held up El Dorado, ready to stamp.

"It makes me do this!" he yelled.

It was glowing white hot and potent in his hand. He reached into his coat pocket and in the same motion exchanged the stamp for Peachy's gun. From the other pocket he produced a narcotic lozenge the size of a large brown marble.

"The egg comes out of the chicken!" he yelled. "This alone will kill me. I'll be eating canned wax beans every day for eternity!"

"Creamed corn," I said.

"The rope and bullet are only insurance!"

Honking cars were screeching to a halt on the roadway behind us. Our crowd was drawing a crowd.

"Don't do it, buddy," a man said behind me. "It's not worth it."

"Yes it is!" Tremolito said.

A woman had stopped and was wringing her hands.

"I know how you feel," she said. "I've been there too."

"No you haven't!"

"Things are gonna get better," someone hollered.

"No they won't!"

Fitch was there with the dipstick from his bike, poking Tremolito in the side.

"A nice spot," he said. "Just let me prick him there once."

"There's no need of that," Gabraham cautioned.

A policeman came running up. He slipped on the wet scaffold and almost fell over the edge. He got up and reached out his hand to Tremolito on the rail.

"It's a long way down, friend," he said, "and that water is..."

"Goodbye cruel world!"

Tremolito hurled the pill in the direction of his mouth, but the wind shifted and blew it past his head entirely. He shook off his disbelief. He raised the gun to his head and fired, but the wind shifted again. He lost his balance and missed. The shot severed the rope and nailed a seagull that happened to be flying past. The rope snapped completely when he tipped back.

As Tremolito tipped back we leaned forward. He regained his balance, then lost it and tipped forward, fanning the gun across the crowd. We ducked. He righted himself again, then fell back completely off the rail. He ended up in the bay, sinking like a false confession.

"He will surface again," Gabraham said.

He did not surface again. The crowd waited and speculated.

"Go get him," Basker said to Midge.

"Fuck that, dude. That water's cold!"

Fitch shouted and pointed to the north. Through the encroaching fog we could barely make out Tremolito's figure on the north shore, crawling like a fresh turd into Marin.

The crowd cheered. The policeman wiped his brow. Our caravan weaved through the mess of parked cars.

Rap 46

WE CHASED HIM NORTH OVER THE MOUNTAINS, where we became stranded at a remote pass in a high altitude snowstorm. We quickly ran out of rations and were forced to eat one of Gabraham's mechanics. His flesh was tender, but in want of a fire. We spent a week cowered in a snow cave.

Gabraham had taken to shaking coffee beans in his hand and tossing them out on the ice to divine some pattern of future events. One day he stopped. He was finished throwing them, he said. The beans now foretold Tremolito's presence.

Providence delivered us a means of escape in the form of a giant white beaver. It came through our camp slapping its tail as it foraged. Luckily Gabraham spoke Beaver. It promised to guide us to safety. We followed it to a stream, which led to a river, which ran down out of the mountains where we regrouped. Then we gave thanks and ate the beaver.

We resumed the chase north to Seattle.

"Seattle?" Fitch said. "I spent a week there one day. All it does is rain."

We began to frequent coffeehouses. Tremolito was close. Overlooking the wharf was Queequeg's Coffee. It was dark inside, and no one looked up as the core of the crusade posse crowded in and shook off the rain.

Tremolito was slunked in a front and corner wooden booth. The interior moisture had condensed on the window, and the shadows falling on his face became tears. In front of him were lined up twenty-one espresso shots. Each shot had a sugar cube and dollar-store spoon on its saucer.

"The most perilous of all the trials," Gabraham said.

"I came here to testify," Tremolito said, "and to give myself up. In twenty-one shots I can take myself and this evil that consumes us out of the equation."

"Where's my board, dude?!" Basker demanded.

"And my bike!"

"What about my hog?"

"Where's my barrel, pardner?"

"Give me one minute," I said. "I am gonna grab a cup of coffee."

I left Tremolito surrounded. Gabraham and Basker were leaning on him. The posse was mingling from tastefully velveteened settees, veloured booths and creaking yet functional wooden chairs. I approached the counter.

"You want to know our specials, don't you? Don't you?" said the girl behind the counter. Her nametag read *Gar.*

"I do now."

"Figures. Our specials are the Curry Latte..." she began, then leaned back and yelled. "Hey Grist, what the fuck is the other special besides the Curry Latte?"

Grist mumbled something from the back room.

"Oh yeah," Gar continued, "and the Salmon Blend. We roast it here."

Tough choice.

"Curry Latte," I said.

Gar raised an eyebrow.

"Curry Latte?"

"Curry Latte."

"Are you sure you want a Curry Latte?"

"Yes, a Curry Latte."

"The Curry Latte's not for everyone. You're sure?"

"Sure."

"A Curry Latte?"

"A Curry Latte."

She hesitated and looked me in the eye.

"Curry Latte?"

"Curry Latte."

"Curry...?"

"Curry..."

We said 'latte' at the same time.

"Alright," she said, "but you gotta have a tat if you want to buy anything here."

I was in luck. I turned and showed her the can opener on my ass.

"Wow, nice scab tat. Ten bucks."

I pulled a soggy twenty out of my pocket.

"Buy yourself one too," I offered.

"I don't drink coffee."

I was staring at the tattoos on her chest.

"Are you looking at my tits?" she said.

"I'm looking at your tats."

"Stop looking at my tats! You must first ask me if you may look at my tats."

"May I look at your tats?"

"You didn't say the magic word."

"What is the magic word?"

"Please."

"Please, may I look at your tats?" I said.

"No," she said, "you may not look at my tits or my tats. Now, fuck off with your fucking Curry Latte."

She handed me my drink. I fucked off. On my way back to the booth I sipped. The buzz hit my crotch with electricity. I took another sip. I could feel my trouser biscotti grow for the first time in weeks. I sipped again. This time my biscotti grew and grew and grew. Then, as unexpected as its growth, it began to whistle.

It whistled a jolly good tune as clear as a marching soldier. Customers smiled and whistled knowingly along as

I passed. When I made it back to the booth I looked at Gar. She blew me a kiss and began to whistle as she wiped the pastry case.

"The pain and suffering of the world is about to come down on you like Caesar's sandal," Gabraham was saying to Tremolito.

"It won't change things," Tremolito said.

"We'll see about that."

Gabraham clapped his hands three times. There was a quick puff of smoke. When the smoke was gone Krist Novaselic was sitting in the booth across from us.

"I am the icing on your frosty cake, punk," Krist said.

"I knew you'd find me eventually," Tremolito said.

"Man, you gotta give it up."

"I don't get it," Basker said.

"I'm not the dude from Nirvana right now. I'm God. Watch, gimmee some bumps. See? Krist would never give you bumps, not in public at least. He'd kick your ass for being such a dork in a coffeehouse."

"You know a barista died here last week?" Tremolito mused, pointing at Gar. "Espresso machine exploded, blew him right out the back door."

"You can't suicide by caffeine," Gabraham said. "You'll only end up on television."

Each sip of the Curry Latte firmed up and advanced the tune of my rejoicing biscotti. I discerned a medley of cartoon and sitcom themes, standards and humdingers, murder ballads and work songs, jazz solos and whip-smart classical arrangements. The whistler became a cheerful soundtrack to the intervention as it piped unseen in my pants.

I pulled Tremolito's empty prescription bottle from my pocket and stamped it on the table. Tremolito pulled El Dorado from his pocket and did the same. Then he knelt before Krist, and turned to Gabraham.

"Oh my captain, my captain, noble heart!" he cried. "Our fearful trip is done."

"The ship is anchored safe, lad," the angel reassured him.

"Enough with the fancy language already!" Fitch said.

Tremolito lifted his head to meditate on the ornately contoured and appropriately walnutted trim along the ceiling.

"For me they call, the swaying mass, their eager faces turning..."

"I have no choice but to do this," Krist said, placing his hand on Tremolito's shoulder. "Just hold still a second."

In a flash of bituminous phosphate he turned Tremolito into a hulking grunge knight wearing a bedraggled flannel shirt, ripped concert tee and muddy hiking boots. His hair now hung to his shoulders.

"The stage is near, the distortion I hear, the kids all moshing..."

Tremolito rose slowly. In a second phosphorescent flash an electric guitar case appeared at his feet. Without saying another word he picked up the case and slung it over his shoulder, then wandered out into the rain and sloping street.

"Hey, who farted?" Basker said.

"'Tis the first foul wind I ever knew to blow from astern," Gabraham said.

"Wait a minute," Fitch said. "Where's that whistling coming from?"

I cupped my hands and covered my biscotti.

"My Captain!" he said.

"Look here, Pop Art," Krist said, "there's been a change of plans. I need you to relinquish your marker. Why? I'll tell you why. I decided to roll with McTuggins instead. When you get back please see that he gets it, capeche?"

Krist reached out and nudged the holy marker.

"Thanks for your service, buddy. No hard feelings, right? You do get the parting gift, though."

He reached his hands out for my head.

"'Scuse me, gentlemen, while I kiss this guy."

They 'scused him. Krist wetted my lips, slobbering and twisting my head.

My biscotti was pounding. I got another Curry Latte and dunked it in the mug under the table. It made bubbles as it whistled. When it was warm it eased over and pointed south. It was time to go home.

As I left I saw the tattoo of a can opener working a can of beans on Krist's arm.

"Are you looking at my tats?" he said.

I bought a pound of Salmon Blend for the road.

Rap 47

BY THE TIME I RETURNED my dreams of Tiger had been washed away by the oil and grit of the highway. I was broker than broke, down once again to my last twenty dollars. I could no longer even claim divinity since God had pulled me out of the game. El Dorado, the holy golden rubber stamp, still awaited passing, but the task was a crude formality.

The crusade to bring the stamp home was finished, but my whistling trouser biscotti remained. Something needed doing. It had grown to three times its length. It was rigid as a broom handle, but no inspiration. Walking was difficult. The boisterous whistling kept me awake at night. I would pass women and be slapped. I would pass men and be slapped. I tried to teach it to type as an eleventh finger, but it lay too heavy on the space bar.

"You could try stroking it," Basker said.

"Dear heavens, no!" Gabraham warned. "You will most certainly go blind."

"Gabe," I said, "I'm over here."

I sat at the typewriter for the first time in weeks. I gave Basker's words a second thought. My pants came off. I developed a quick fantasy of my typewriter in cotton panties and began to work it. After a few strokes the room suddenly went black. I stood and stumbled back, reaching for the light. I waved my hands in front of my face. Nothing. Now I had done it.

I would need a miracle. I would need immaculate intervention. I would need a cigarette. I fumbled for my pack and lighter. I lifted one to my face, but in my blindness jammed it up my nose. I took a deep breath. On my second try I got the booger-encrusted cigarette to my lips but it was backwards. When the fire touched the filter the flameout swelled my lips. The cigarette was destroyed, but the explosion had returned my sight. Indeed, it was a lesson in miracles.

Every good miracle deserves wine. The thought of the grapes stained any absence of shame. Twenty dollars buys a lot of wine. I pulled on my pants both legs at a time.

They were barely over my ankles when the thought hit me. I would keep El Dorado. I could hide him away where he would never be found. Only I would know how to cross the golden frontier as it stormed and beckoned awaiting my command. My character would be boundless. Answers to questions never asked would be revealed. Questions never answered would be asked. Dogs would fuck cats, and I would write about it. I could disappear to an island with palm trees, sunshine, groves of cigarettes, terraced marijuana fields, tide pools of Golden's strange brew, and an Olivetti Lettera typewriter in edible cotton panties. God would never find me.

That did not last long. From far off I heard the sound of wings gathering air. Not many, just two. They were fast approaching. They circled twice over the garage, then the rogue neighborhood parrot flew in the window and landed on the typewriter. He reached his beak out for the Whistler but I slapped him away.

He turned and leaned into the keys. He typed one letter at a time, pecking the keys to spell out a word. When he finished he hit the return bar, then flew to the windowsill. I looked down at what he had typed. There was only one word, a name.

"McTuggins."

I looked again and the parrot was gone.

I pressed the biscotti to my stomach so I could pull on my pants. El Dorado was always in my pocket. The twenty was in my otherwise empty wallet, which was also in my pocket. Loaded and ready for wine time. I could find McTuggins, pass the stamp like bad gas, and be ready for a fine time. I hurried up the street.

Of all the luck. Parked in front of the Evening Wood Nursing Home was Miguel. I could see the pimp ice cream truck in the distance. He was a longshot. If he could rip out a cure for the Whistler, his price would be right. McTuggins could wait.

"My friend," Miguel said, sitting up, "como estas?"

"No mucho."

He laughed so hard he spit crumbs.

"Har, har harrrrr. No mucho! Har, hee, hee, hee."

He was eating an ice cream sandwich and moist, black cookie flesh was ground by his howling teeth before falling from his mouth.

"Always you keed, my friend. The last time you left you was running up the street."

"It was the angels."

"Ah, si," he remembered. "God told me."

He wiped the ice cream spooge from his chin, and made the sign of a cross.

"We did coffee," I said.

I thought about it for a second.

"In Seattle."

"Why have you come today, my friend? La mota? Cigars? Diet pills?"

"No."

"Pescado fresco?"

"No."

"Pescado fragrante?"

"No."

"Pescado foochy?"

"No."

"Menudos para Los Cruzados?"

"No."

He hesitated.

"What, jou need a gun?"

I hesitated.

"No, no gun."

"Tequila?"

"No."

"El pulque?"

"No."

"Chingon bracelets?"

"No."

"Chicas underpants?"

"No."

He smiled and leaned toward me.

"Un favor?"

"No."

"Un favor poco?"

"No."

"Un favor poquito?"

"No."

"Un favor poquito-ito?"

"No."

"Si, un favor!" he insisted.

"No, no favor."

He thought for a moment.

"You don't want no ice cream, do you?"

"No."

"Ees good, 'cause I just ate the last pinche sandwich," he said, licking his fingers. "So, my friend, what the fuck you want, anyway? Just say and I will get for you."

"I need something for this," I said, dropping trou. The Whistler fell out of my shorts like a drawbridge.

Miguel leaned out the window of his truck for a better look.

"I cannot make eet larger."

"It needs to be smaller," I said, "and quieter."

"No comprendo."

I reached above my head and grabbed the truck's awning. I pulled myself up so my waist was closer to his eye level. The Whistler cleared his tube, and ran up and down C major. He broke into a quick medley of surf cumbias before I had to let go.

"I see," Miguel said, nodding, "but I cannot help you with thees problem."

He disappeared into the truck and came back flipping through the pages of an ancient leather bound book. There were spiders clinging to this book, and it smelled older than dirt. He ran his finger down a page. He stopped and studied. Finally he closed the book.

"Eet ees as I suspect. You need El Amor Grande."

"No, anything but that."

"You need the Big Love."

I raised the drawbridge and closed the castle walls.

"Someone needs to take eet away for you."

"I see."

I ended up buying a dimebag while I was there. He had to borrow my pen, but he wrote the address of a Tijuana whorehouse on his discarded ice cream sandwich wrapper.

"Good luck with your churro mariachi, my friend."

He shook a hang-loose and a thumbs-up at the same time. I was facing the truck when he pulled away. When he pulled away I was facing Evening Wood. There was a burning steamroller bong hovering at the front door. The door opened by itself and the bong floated inside. The time had come to pass the marker.

I crossed the street and hesitated at the open door. A cold, dry wind blew from inside. The hairs on my scrot tingled. I thought of running with El Dorado in the opposite direction. My heart raced. I took a thousand-mile step.

Inside I was met by a trio of long, empty corridors. They were caverns of bleached linoleum. The light above my head flickered. To my left I saw the bong at the end of a hall. I drove a cigarette to my lips, and before I could reach for my lighter it fired up on its own. I puffed, and it tasted real.

Also real was the smell of accreted urine which knocked me back on my haunches. It was a bionic cider, an aging olfactory minstrel dancing around my head. Even the tobacco smoke could not frustrate the smell. It was a forest of odor, a wilderness of decay that only thickened the further down the hall I went. Cries and moans and whispers of strange and wounded beasts emanated from the rooms as I passed. There was a nurse's station ahead, a settlement to regain my values. The bong had disappeared, but I was too far in to quit. The only way back was forward.

I braced myself on the counter. There was a sink, and I splashed some cold water on my face. El Dorado was draining my strength. I might not make it to McTuggins. I called out his name, but the cigarette in my lips made it sound like "Maggugginnziz!"

I withdrew it and called out again.

"McTuggins!"

The name was absorbed into the walls.

"McTuggins!"

The cigarette went back in my mouth without a fight. Silently I smoked, until the silence was rent by what sounded like a cricket rubbing one out. Maybe it was an elbow joint extending for the first time in weeks, then the faint sound of someone's hand carefully opening and spelunking a deep desk drawer. McTuggins, I thought. There was an open office door behind me. Slowly I turned.

The name on the door was "Annabelle Lector, R.N." Kicked back on the far side of the desk in the dark office I could see an Evening Wood resident permanently reclined in a wheelchair. Her face was sallow and drawn and caught a dusty sliver of light that managed to find its way between the closed draperies. Her eyes were vacated, if not demented, aged and cheddared with weeks of goo damming her tear ducts, gazing up into a corner of the ceiling. Her right hand, however, had somehow opened and was working its way through Nurse Lector's unlocked meds drawer.

Perfect timing. McTuggins would have to wait. I tiptoed in and looked over her shoulder. It was like watching someone masturbate in their sleep. I saw the tendons in her forearm tighten as her hand hooked something and slowly pulled out. From the meds drawer I expected a syringe or bottle of pills. Instead she pulled a dainty squeeze-bottle of nasal spray.

It took only a hot second to realize that the nasal spray contained smephedrine, a powerful amphetamine used to revive horses that have overdosed on tranquilizer. I knew this because the bottle was plain white except for the large words "Smephedrine: Dangerous" printed on the side. Available by prescription only, it was highly addictive and hard to come by. It also had aphrodisiac qualities that made it uniquely prized among professional writers of quality pornographic letters.

With the dexterity of a blind jeweler she undid the cap with one hand and two fingers, and raised the bottle to the vicinity of her nose, missing both nostrils. The bottle filled with air and she tried again, but the desire in her grip was so strong the bottle wheezed with pneumatic phlegm, shooting a tiny fountain of decongestant into the air in a mad snoring rhythm.

My tongue began massaging the roof of my mouth. Precious smephedrine was being wasted before my very eyes. A miracle was needed. I reached out to delicately poach the spray bottle from her hand.

"I'm sorry, sir, but you can't smoke in here."

The sudden voice in the doorway behind me clenched my organs. My fingers stopped in mid-snatch, inches from the spray. Slowly I turned. There appeared before me a crescent moon of a nurse, as young and precious as anticipated snow.

"You'll have to extinguish your cigarette, or step out onto our lovely smoking terrace just off the dining area, where you can find many places to dispose of your soon-to-be-discarded nicotine delivery device."

I had forgotten the cigarette dangling from my lips. I took a final drag and handed it to the nurse. Before she touched it I pulled it back and took a second final drag, then handed it over. I reconsidered again and pulled it back for a third, fourth, fifth and sixth final drag before relinquishing. When she went out to dowse it in the sink at the nurse's station I acted quick to pinch the nasal spray from the old woman's hand.

I twisted and pulled but she would not give it up. Her abandoned lips curled and her eyebrows shook as she fought me. Her constrained emotions were seismic. I had to slap her hand finally to emancipate the spray. Her head wilted and for a moment our eyes locked, then she looked away. The nurse was throwing my soggy butt into the biohazard container. I lifted the smephedrine spray to my nose for a quick squirt, but squeezed it too hard. The bottle was wet and shot over my head in a graceful arc onto the floor.

"Oh my goodness, did you get that nasal decongestant from Mrs. Jones?" The nurse picked up the bottle from the floor. "You may have just saved her life! This spray contains a powerful and addictive stimulant called smephedrine. See?"

She held up the bottle of danger. I saw.

"Mrs. Jones is the only one on this floor whose fragile health precludes her from using it. If she inhaled even a drop it could give her a myocardial infarction."

"Excuse you?"

She pulled a tray from the meds drawer. The tray was

completely mustered with plain white nasal spray bottles identical to the one I had pinched from Mrs. Jones. There might have been fifty or more. My heart skipped a beat. I caught my breath. I could write an entire set of dirty novels powered by all that smephedrine. She counted the sprays with her fingertips and filled the deficit made by Mrs. Jones. The tray went back in the drawer.

"Dear me, Nurse Annabelle must have left her medicine drawer unlocked. She's always warning me about the consequences of this sort of thing happening. I can't imagine what would happen if someone had gotten in there with ideas to use this proper, legal medicine for reasons other than its intended purpose."

Her excessive ethics and florid tongue brought forth lurid images from the turgid pool of my brain. I imagined her scolding me in front of my typewriter and making it type on its own. Yet she continued.

"I mean, gosh, an innocent resident like Mrs. Jones who finds her way in here, or visiting grandkids just wanting to clear their nasal passages, or, heaven forbid, a writer of pornographic letters could be wandering our halls looking for unlocked nurse's drawers to raid to get high and feed their socially pathological smephedrine addictions."

She closed the drawer but did not lock it.

"They're the worst. So needy and evasive, almost wormlike. We get three or four of those writer creeps a month wandering around looking to loot our proper and legal smephedrine nasal spray. You're not a writer, are you?"

The syllables rolled off her tongue, and filled the room with the question of questions. My hand instinctively went for the trusty pen always alert in my hip pocket. It was gone. I felt deeper and found the whorehouse number Miguel had written on the ice cream wrapper. He was probably halfway to Tijuana with my pen.

"I don't even have a pen."

She produced a pen from her uniform pocket and handed it to me.

"There, now you're a writer. Wanna buy some smeph?"

"Sure."

The meds drawer opened again. She pulled a vacuum-sealed freshie from the ranks.

"Ten bucks each."

My last ten was handed over for a chance to burn up the page.

"I'm Polly, but you can call me Polly."

"Okay, Polly."

"No, just Polly."

"Good golly, Miss Polly."

It got better. From my equator there drifted the whistle I had come to know so well.

"Oh my, what in ever could be that sound?" said Nurse Polly before gasping. "Someone's whistling!"

He had picked up on my allusion and was belting out Little Richard.

"Aww, how quaint," she added. "Oh, hello, Nurse Annabelle!"

At first Polly's words did not make sense.

"Nurse, how many times have I told you to address me by my proper title?"

"I'm sorry, Nurse Lector, I forgot."

With one sentence Annabelle Lector put the 'nurse' in nursing home. She crept into her now-crowded office with the dignity of a grieving toreador and a sun-dried tomato of a nose. There was a mysterious thatch of fuzzy head-nurse scurvy hanging from her lower lip that quivered even though the room was still. The Whistler fell dumb in the air conditioned hum of her voice.

"Nurse Purple, please tell me why you are not at your station, and spending your valuable time in my office with this, this, this..."

I was indescribable.

"...this, this, this..."

I was still indescribable.

"...this, this, this...backwoodsman!"

It must have been the beard. I had not shaved since Thanksgiving. I had not combed it either. Polly covered.

"Nurse Lector, this is Mrs. Jones' loving and adoring son."

"Really? I wasn't aware that Mrs. Jones..."

She leaned in.

"...had a son!"

The sun-dried tomato was right in my face.

"We've hardly spoken," I said.

"Mr. Jones just saved the life of his dear sweet mother when he prevented her from taking the wrong medication from your unlocked medication drawer, which could have had terrible consequences and might have even caused a myocardial infarction."

"Excuse you?"

Nurse Lector looked at Polly holding the ten, then at the open meds drawer. Then she looked at me, and finally to the prostituted smephedrine nasal spray in my hand. The sun-dried tomato began to flare with impatience.

"There's something happening here, Mr. Jones, but I don't know what it is. I intend to find out. Nurse Purple, I'd like a word with you."

I waited for the word to fall.

"Alone! Mr. Jones, please wait outside while I speak with Nurse Purple!"

The door hit me on the way out. I looked left. I looked right. I broke the seal and took a quick civil snort of smeph hunched in a corner next to a fire extinguisher. The rush hit my brain immediately, and felt ten times better than when I had once huffed a bongload of gasoline at a party on someone's balcony overlooking the beach.

"Hey, Rain Man! Let's go, I got shit to do!"

The voice was coming from a door at the end of the hall. After a second quick inhale I found myself hesitating at the threshold, then pushing on through.

I was in the kitchen. The steam tables stank of boiling gristle and pureed hot dogs.

"Hairnet."

I had just missed lunch.

"Hairnet!!"

A small cardboard box filled with white nylon hairnets bounced off the side of my head. I bent down and pulled one from the box. The tosser was chopping lettuce with a cleaver. It was the cook.

"I'm looking for McTuggins."

The cook raised the cleaver high and drove it deep into the cutting board.

"McTuggins!" she hollered into the dish room. She turned back to me. "I told him no probation officers."

"I'm not a probation officer."

She turned to call.

"McTuggins! Your probation officer is here again! I told you no visits on the clock!"

She turned back to me.

"I told him no probation officers."

I found McTuggins in the dish room. His hairnet was unable to cover the fern of dreads that hung over his face. I watched as he took the dirty plates from the serving trays and sprayed them with the sink hose. Without a wash or dry he placed them in the plate warmer for the next meal. He used his wet hands to stroke his hair back after each dish, and after each stroke it would fall over his face again.

I tapped him on the shoulder.

"Hey bro, deliveries are through the kitchen."

"This is a special delivery," I said.

I mistakenly pulled the bottle of smephedrine from my pocket and handed it to him.

"Thanks dude, but I got, like, a thousand of those at home."

He handed it back and returned to the dishes. I tapped him on the shoulder.

"Deliveries are through the kitchen."

This time I pulled El Dorado from my pocket and held it up just long enough to gain his attention. His attention gained I lifted his hand and opened his palm. With my pinkie raised I delicately set the marker in his hand and closed his fingers around it.

"Aw thanks, dude. I've always wanted one of these."

He looked it over.

"What the fuck is it?"

"That is a myocardial infarction."

"Excuse you?"

"That is a you-know-what."

He turned it over and tried to remove the gold handle.

"Where's the carb?"

"That is no pipe. It is a gift from you-know-who."

He looked at El Dorado. He rolled it around his brain, and again looked at El Dorado in his hand. He looked at me and pointed to the sky. I nodded. He smiled.

"Dude, no way," he said.

"Way."

He left the water running in the sink as he wandered around the dish room in a daze. He shook his head and started to say 'dude, no way' but only his lips moved. He laughed to himself. He looked at me.

"Dude, no way."

"Way."

The back door blew open with a sudden wind.

"McTuuugggiinnnnsss..." the wind said.

McTuggins dragged his knuckles across the room, and the sunlight refracted off El Dorado in his hand. His entire being seemed to glow.

"McTuuugggiinnnnsss..."

He stepped down the walk in coronation. From out of nowhere rose petals blew into his path, leading him to the street. There were cars coming fast and hard from both directions. It was surely a suicide to be seen, not heard.

Just as he was about to become his own ghost the cars stopped, and the afternoon marine layer parted above his head. A light brighter than the sun shone down from the sky. Krist was hanging from a rafter of clouds, and held out his hand.

"No fucking way,"

"Way," Krist said. "C'mon up, bro!"

"I fucking love California!"

"No fucking way," I said.

Krist snapped his fingers and the pair ascended into the sky. A nylon hairnet drifted down from the clouds like a clinical white jellyfish, and an astonished woman rushed out into the street to grab it before it touched the ground. She sniffed it and kissed it, then stuffed it in her bra and looked around before running away.

It felt like I was walking on water. I was. The sink was flowing over. I needed stability. My hand patted the cigarettes in my pocket. I went through McTuggins' hemp wallet that I found above the sink and came up with a few coins and small bills, as well as a crumpled but smokable pinner joint.

I had made it. I was free. I stepped outside and sparked up.

Rap 48

THE PINNER WAS A DUD. I twisted it apart and sniffed a faint mixture of oregano and basil. It was an herbal slugfest. I had no plans to season anything so I tossed the two halves of the demi-joint on the ground. My foot was about to crush the imposters when I noticed a wide trail of ants moving across the terrace. Their destination was a pair of shoed feet about ten feet away. The feet were sticking out from behind a brick wall that divided the smoking terrace from that of mere mortals. I peered around the bricks.

It was him, yes him, the old man with the shock of white hair who watched always my misfortune from his chair. There he was again, his peckish beak accusing me from the front of his face, his blue eyes searing my soul with their vacuity. He was a stone outcropping on the bald face of Mount Whatever. He sat there and stared at me like Revelations gone wrong.

I pulled the bottle of smeph from my pocket and held it up for him to see. I moved it from side to side, but it was like offering paint to a brick wall. Nada. He even declined to decline. I took matters into my own hands and gave him a quick blast in each shaggy nostril. I scarfed the next hit, and the next after that. The stim hit my brain and my knees buckled.

For a moment nothing moved. The porch vibrated with a speedy chrome luster. I steadied myself on his chair. Two grains of basmati rice dripping with smephedrine crawled out of his nose. I shook my head. They fought and crawled over each other all the way to his ear where they reentered the warmth of his head.

It was then I noticed the smell. It was the same smell as a dead raccoon I had seen along some railroad tracks as a child, but he was no raccoon. Not yet, anyway. I fired up a stog.

The trail of ants was working its way from the porch to his shoes and up the legs of his pants. They were eating him, piece by bitsy piece, bite by itsy bite. I could hear them, mandibles by the thousands. It was a banquet of the tiny. They were louder than the birds. Flies that had been buzzing around his head now began circling around mine. I placed my burning cigarette between his fingers, and backed across the grass to the sidewalk.

I walked with an ugly confidence. I was Manson before the desert, ready to go bald and bearded as Bustoff at a moment's notice. I was myth, meme and archetype. I was the sand ever shifting. I caught my reflection in a tinted van window. The rips of smeph had given me the eight-ball eyes of a cornered fox. I slapped myself in the face. Eight-balls in the side pocket.

The pep was in my step. Birds alighted on my shoulders and sang. The Whistler led the tune to the rhythm of my cowboy swagger. He twiddled all the walking songs from Fats to Patsy, and made up a couple of his own. I was my own marching band, boogie incarnate, at least until the man waiting at the bus stop fifty paces ahead turned at the sound of my parade.

It was as if I had lived the moment before. Lo, he was the same milquetoast Peachy had pummeled on Christmas, standing in the exact same spot of that yuletide beat-down. His pluck posture was supported by a crutch, and draped like a toga over his frame was a sleeping bag. He was wearing a fatigued army jacket, full of homelessness and certainly ripe to the nose. He was sure to remember me and exact revenge.

I slowed, then quickened my pace to fake him out.

"Hey buddy," he said, "check it out. You wanna..."

"Here comes the bus," I said, looking down the street.

He turned to see the bus.

"Aww, that's just a garbage truck. Hey, wait a minute. I know you."

He stuck the crutch in my path.

"Wait, you kicked my ass on Christmas!"

His verbs calcified in my ears. He was shorter than I remembered, and with the crutch extended from his arm it made him look like he was on stilts. He jammed the crutch into his armpit and his hand reached into his coat. I pivoted, but his other hand caught my arm. I was to be stabbed for sure. He would shove a knife in my side, and they would find me hanging from the rafter of the bus shelter.

"Hey, don't worry man, I'm not mad or nuthin'. I always wanted to say thanks for kicking my ass back then. I really needed it, and boy did I deserve it, all the shit I've done. Flamethrowers and Saigon prostitutes don't mix, that's for goddamn sure."

He produced from his jacket not a knife but the largest marijuana torpedo I had ever seen, almost the length of his forearm and nearly as fat. It was a fifty-year spliff, a hooter you might encounter once every half-century. Its construction easily involved a hundred rolling papers.

I began coughing.

"Wow, you okay, buddy?"

He moved to pat my back. I flinched and choked up a drip of smeph that had fallen from my sinus to my throat.

"So I got laid up in the infirmary in a half-body cast for a month after that beating. Thing is, for the pain they had nurses feed me the best medical marijuana the government grows. Can you believe it? The nurse would do everything, grind, roll, put it in my mouth and light it. All I had to do was lay there and smoke."

The man had somehow lived my dream, everything except the part about getting his ass kicked.

"This shit made me so high I thought I was back in Cambodia smoking that Thai stick. They told me it helped my body heal fifty percent faster. This was doctors tellin' me this shit! I got out last week and they gave me a fresh pound of it on prescription, just put it in my arms as I was walking out the door, and they were like, 'have a nice day!'"

Dude definitely had my dream.

"They call it Forest Preserve. It's a hydro, so they don't actually grow it in the woods, but once you smoke it you'll feel like you're a tree."

He held one end of the bomber under my nose and dragged it lengthwise for what seemed to be an eternity, at least ten seconds from one twist to the other. It was the best ten seconds of my life. I had to add this to the stash of dimebag, smeph and smokies already laden in my pants. I felt a wadded dollar bill in my pocket.

"Fifty cents," I said.

"Fifty cents?" he whined. "This is worth at least a monthly transit pass, like fifty bucks."

I remembered how Peachy had manhandled him. I upped.

"Okay, a dollar."

I pulled the crumpled dollar from my pocket.

"Aw, you gotta go higher than that," he said.

I held the bill high above his head. He began jumping to grab it. Each time he would jump I would raise it another couple of inches.

"Aw, c'mon man. Don't play games. I know I'm short."

He kept jumping. I took the bomber from his hand and pushed him. He staggered, then came back. I pushed his other shoulder and he staggered again, this time the crutch giving way beneath him. I breast-pocketed the torpedo. Freedom takes the sucker every time. I handed him the dollar.

"Fuck, I guess so, man. This shit ain't right."

I pulled out Polly's magic pen.

"Here is a note for the other forty-nine dollars."

I wrote on the whorehouse ice cream wrapper the words 'other forty-nine dollars' and handed it to him.

"Aww, thanks buddy. You'd do that for me?"

"Sure."

"I don't know how to thank you."

"I do."

I started to walk past him, my redwood spliff hip to dip in the wine that would soon be mine, but his crutch came to my knees in toll.

"This means so much to me."

"Me too," I said, backing up while eyeing the crutch.

"Yeah, guess I'll see you around, huh? I mean, I hope so,

you're so cool and all."

I turned, ready to skitch a long way around the block.

"You're, like, my hero."

"Super."

"Hey, before you go can I ask you a question?"

I waved over my shoulder.

"You just did."

"I see the pen. Are you a writer?"

Crosses are hewn to be worn. Again there was the question, twice in one day. My stride died and my body locked. My face clenched in a rictus, my throat emitting a squeaky gasp before my chin fell to my chest.

"I have no choice."

He looked from side to side in broad daylight.

"Then, hey, I got somethin' else you might be interested in."

He opened his coat. There was a rolled up porno called "Fingered" screwed into the inside pocket. It was a glossy monthly, neophytes caught in the act of typing in their birthday suits. To have a letter published in "Fingered" meant the market's bottom had been not only scraped, but also penetrated. Perusal of the periodical was just as piercing.

"Just add five to this note and we'll call it even."

Hesitation took a nosedive as he waved the porno in my face. I pulled out the pen to write 'five' on the lewd and creamy wrapper. This time the smeph was pulled out with it. The little white squeezy bottle fell to the sidewalk and bounced a couple of times before rolling to his feet.

"Whoa, what's that?"

I prepared a speech of self-righteousness.

"That is a myocard..."

"Wait, I know what that is!"

I knew where he was headed. Smephedrine meant different things to different people. An unrepentant pedophile had recently been arrested living in a den of empty smeph bottles. When the police counted them all it was more than a hundred-thousand, all spent. The case had gained a degree of notoriety and been in the headlines for the past year. The man on the crutch bent to pick up the smeph.

"No, I don't know what it is."

He paused. He paused so long I could hear a piano somewhere in the neighborhood. Again I turned to leave.

"Wait, yes, I do."

He hopped back a step on the crutch. Shameful words were forming on the crest of his lips.

"I'll bet you're one of them perverted writers!"

He was right, but for the wrong reasons.

"You're a goddamn child molester!"

Even a prophet of circumstance could not have predicted what happened next.

Our bus stop standoff was across the street from the parking lot behind St. Ignatius. St. Ignatius just happened to have a world-class boys choir, and as Crutch Man's words rang up and down the West Coast a harem of those choirboys in full vestment was loading a church van not forty feet away. The van was parked behind a chain link fence, and there were twelve or thirteen boys whose ears suddenly perked, and whose eyes tendered the sight of blood. The call for revenge was about to be slaked.

One vaulted a fire plug. Another boy threw off his frock to reveal a pair of nun-chucks, which he started whirling. A couple of brawny lads tore through the chain link fence. They came at me like angry Christmas ornaments. Before I could understand the what of the situation I was surrounded by the pubescent acolytes from St. Ignatius. They had crossed the street quicker than a confession, and their wafer-delicate hands were stretching for my throat, their war-cries trembling like Gregorian birdcalls. Instinctively I drew the pen and crouched in defense.

"Wow," the tallest boy said, "calling all badasses. What're you gonna do with that pen, Hemingway?"

I stabbed quick at his face to answer his question. The crowd gave me some room. They began circling. My accuser was using his crutch for pitchfork jabs at my sweetbreads. I parried with the pen, clicking the ballpoint in and out at a menacing clip. I went on the offensive and stabbed forth with no delay, but lunged too far. The tall boy caught my forearm with a judo chop and smartly depenned me.

He spun me around and held the pen to my throat.

"Whaddya say, now, Hemingway? How does it feel to be a little homeward angel?"

"That was...Wolfe," I gagged.

"Wolfe stole it from Milton," another boy spat.

I was knee-deep in no-goodness. The boy dragged me by the neck for about three feet with the pen still poised over my jugular. I felt him rummaging through my pockets, but was outnumbered.

"Holy shit, this gimp's a gumball machine!"

He dispensed the contents of my pockets to the mob.

"Some small bills, heavy change, nice fat sack, and what is this? Some smokies?"

"I'll take those," said a lad of about seven.

"No!"

I broke free and there was another standoff.

"Your shoe is untied," I said.

They all looked down. In the diversion I made like I was going to spin and bolt, but my foot caught on a tectonic piece of sidewalk. My arms flew forward so fast they could not prevent my face from smacking the concrete. A sting of pain and a sudden swallow of blood told my nose it was broken for sure. My eyes flitted.

I knew I was still alive because you can't steal from the dead. Crutch Man reached down and took the bomber from my shirt pocket.

"I'll just be taking that back."

Through my flitting lids I saw the tall boy push and snarl at Crutch Man. Crutch Man leered back like a cool coyote. The tall boy claimed me.

"Step back, Tripod. This one belongs to us."

The boy had a look I would call crazy. His eyes began twitching in an ecstatic dance as he bent over me.

"Good morning, little schoolgirl," he said.

He wasted no time in ripping off my pants and throwing them in the street. The other boys began loosening their belts. Suddenly all the dogs in the neighborhood began barking. There was fresh meat in the cell block.

"The hounds of hell!" the seven-year-old whispered, dropping the smokes.

"Leave the child molester!" said the tall boy, throwing

the pen on my chest.

"Run for your motherfucking lives!" Crutch Man said, kicking me one last time, hard and swift before limping away on his crutch.

The ruffians scattered like psalms, and for a moment there was silence. From around the corner there approached at a gallop four legs of untrimmed and chewed toenails clicking faster than castanets on the concrete. I imagined two-hundred pounds of apocalyptic dogflesh from the terrible smell of distemper that preceded him. As he neared his breath heaved through salivated jowls, spitting snot, hate and the blood of virgins.

I drew a breath and played possum. I felt his teeth firm around my throat. As his grip tightened my eyes were squeezed open from the force of his vise.

"Of all the..."

It was Tipsy, returned from exile to rescue me from the wraithlike revengers.

"Tids…Tirs…Tips…" I gurgled.

My words spattered in the air. His grip tightened ever so slightly before releasing.

"Ruff, ruff-ruff-ruff. Awwwrrr, ruff?" he asked.

"Pants..."

Some dogs wear a whiskey keg for rescue operations. Tipsy wore a fatty ganja turd that was crooked as Ichabod Crane on crack. He brought my pants, adding a patina of saliva to the ass-crack hem, then turned his backside to my face. There was a message tied to his balls. I reached up and untied the blue silk ribbon rigging the missive to his manly handbags. As I pulled on his balls Tipsy farted. It smelled like rotten eggs and radish piss. I choked up a malodorous blurb of bile, and unrolled the message. It was a page of paw prints. It read:

"Moving to Alaska ... stop ... sled dogging ... stop ... tell Jack ... stop ..."

Tipsy's thugs were waiting for him at the top of the hill. He ran to join them, turning for a brief moment in heroic pose. Then they disappeared over the crest faster than a howling pack of lies.

I was alone on the sidewalk. The bus stop was vacant.

There was no traffic. Not sure if Tipsy was a dream, but the message was in one hand and the ganja turd was in the other. I scraped across the sidewalk blindly and found my lighter. I sparked up, and lay there and looked at the sky.

I finished the turd before attempting to stand. My face felt like a fresh woodcut. I circled in a daze, unsure if I was headed for home. I wiped a mess of blood from my eyes, and evicted more from my nose onto someone's grass. People avoided me as I stumbled.

My huevos locos were aching, but somehow my trouser churro, my mariachi jalapeno of song, the Waist-High Whistling Whistler of the West, was hanging low again. Low and soft and kind of to the left. A dribble of pee escaped his puckered nostril. It wasn't the Big Love I had expected, but under the circumstances it did the trick. It was again silent and at peace.

When I got to the front step there was a note in Veronica's handwriting stuck under a rock.

"It's just you and me baby," it said. "Conquer the world! Love and other things, Veronica."

She was coming around to my point of view. Exactly on her way home, once and for all times.

In the end the pen was truly mightier than the sword, but sometimes a sword is just a pen. I sat on the front step and hosed the blood off my face in the front yard. The surfboard cancelled me out, vibrating in the hum of the afternoon.

I reached into my pocket. My keys were gone. I would have to jump the fence.

It wasn't my house but it was home.

Rap 49

THE NEXT AFTERNOON I WOKE and made myself a cup of Salmon Blend. Jack was rubbing sauce on a rack of ribs. They looked better than my face. I touched them. They felt better as well. I sniffed them. You know they smelled better. They sizzled.

"There's a letter from Tipsy," I said.

"Read it to me."

The letter said we could find him outside Dawson in the Yukon. He would be leading a team of sled dogs for a courier service in the high, white wilderness bordering Alaska. There had just been a week of fresh powder, twenty feet at the higher elevations, and the team was ready to run hard. He promised to come back and visit once the snow pack melted. I folded the letter and set it on the kitchen counter.

"He's got more balls than both of us put together," Jack said, a reverent tear filling his eye.

I sipped my coffee and sat on the couch. I decided I would write a novel. It would be about...

The screen door rattled with a knock.

"Who is there?"

I could see a shadow through the screen, but there was no response. I fished for a butt. None were worth lighting. I stood, defenseless and naked except for the coffee.

A desert-skinned girl about twenty years old was on the porch. She cradled a swaddled infant in her arms. She looked up at me and smiled.

"I did not think you would still be here," she said. "Please, may I come in? The sun is so bright."

I opened the door. It had been almost a year since I had seen her. She had spent a night with me and her friend in the garage. I still did not know her name.

Instinctively my hand drew to my mouth, but neither held a cigarette. I went into the garage. The girl followed. I pulled the last butt from the pack and sparked it up. She moved closer in the dim light. Her right eye was bruised and black, and she rocked the child gently back and forth before holding him out for me to see.

"He is beautiful, no? His name is Jesus because he was born on Christmas Day," she said, smiling broadly, swaying slowly, "but I call him Chuy."

She looked at me.

"He is your son."

I dragged on the cigarette. I looked at little Chuy barely awake in his mother's arms. He was emboldened against the world by his dreams. I knew he was mine.

"He is yours because you were my first," she said, turning her face to the side, "and only."

Chuy was silent and sleeping to the softness of his mother's voice.

"I don't..." she started, "...I cannot care for him. Father Patricio told me I had to have him. The nurses at the hospital said he could be adopted by people who would care for him and love him." She turned from me. "But I cannot give him away. He is too beautiful."

She turned back to me.

"You see? He knows who you are."

He knew. I knew that he knew. He knew that I knew that he knew. I looked at him sleeping in her arms. The garage was filled with emptiness. She reached up with a finger to wipe a tear from her swollen eye, but it was tender and she had no choice but to let the hesitant drop run off the end of her nose onto Chuy's blanket.

"My father beat me for him. He was jealous and said to go. I stay with my cousins but they say not for long. My father says get rid of him because he is a bastard, but I tell him 'no, he is not...'"

Here she paused long.

"...because he has you."

She sobbed once and choked, but stopped herself.

"My mother will not speak to me. I am alone and...I don't know what to do."

She looked at Chuy sleeping in her arms.

"Will you care for him with me?"

She held him out to me.

"Please, he is beautiful. You cannot say no."

I looked at her and Chuy long enough for my ears to ring. I puffed, then stubbed the last of my cigarette. She looked down at him.

"He is beautiful."

She rocked slow as tobacco smoke on a windless day, a bough in the almost breeze. I could hear wheels on the freeway, its impulsive rush beyond the garage door. Children were playing somewhere up the street, and a kind of lyrical bird was singing just above the roof of the house. I could hear a carpenter hammering.

The girl moved past me and laid Chuy down on my mattress. She stepped back for a moment to see him there, then raised my pillow and lowered it over his sleeping body.

Nothing was said. The pillow was pressed, there was resolution. I heard a car drive by slowly. Jack opened the oven door in the kitchen. The Salmon Blend stewed in the pot. Somewhere a horse bolted from a gate.

After a few moments with the pillow it was over. The child's lungs had burst. She picked him up. He was motionless. Chuy was gone.

"He is beautiful," she whispered.

Her eyes had run dry of tears. They were glazed and distant. Looking into them was like watching human figures parting through a window frozen by a sheet of ice. She moved past me and danced slowly with Chuy, meandering, waltzing to a movement the name of which only she knew.

I followed her into the kitchen. My hands rested on the corners of the frame and I hung in the doorway. Jack's rack of ribs cooled on the stove.

The girl stopped when she reached the stove and sniffed the air.

"I am so hungry."

With her free hand she pulled at a rib on the end of the rack. In her grip the ribs angered the greasy pan.

"Please, you will hold your son."

She handed Chuy to me without taking her eyes off the ribs, reaching for them with both hands. She was eager to get at the animal in the cage. The oven shook with regrets under the fatted pan. Jack leaned back ever so slowly in his chair in the other room.

"Those are, um, better with some sauce."

The girl was too busy for Jack's sauce. She no longer wanted the rib on the end either, her desert-skinned fingers now ripping and tearing to get a tender pair of bars in the middle. I could not resist.

I switched Chuy to my other arm and reached in to help. As we tore the rack in half I lifted three meaty bones to my mouth and gnashed. After two bites my lips and nose were covered in honeyed crimson sauce, and I swallowed too fast, coughing and spraying a squadron of barbecue snot from my nose. I spit a sliver of bone onto the counter, then picked it up and used it to pry a stringy elbow of fat from where it had become stuck between two teeth.

As I plucked my ivories the stubborn rib gristle was ejected upwards at an arcing distance of two or three feet to the side. It bounced off the cupboard after adhering there for a tantalizing second, twirled and fell downward at a feather's pace that defied time and gravity, and tacked fast like a booger onto Chuy's tender noggin. I left the bones in my mouth to peel it from his forehead.

It was then I saw for the first time his scallywag of a spit curl. It was a curl not unlike one I had sported as a hideous love child. Going to brush his aside I discovered it shiny and glued to his brow. Then something occurred to me, which I thought about. After brief consultation with myself something else occurred to me and I jumped back, ribs still in my mouth.

With the sudden movement of my body Chuy's eyes batted open and closed in an arrested, mechanical kind of way. Maneuvering my teeth and tongue so that I would not have to remove the ribs from my mouth I took a speculative bite. His eyes repeated their flip with each gum-smacking chew. Something was rotten in Metropolis.

I poked Chuy's nose. It was slick and hard as a saddle horn. I flicked it with my fingertip as if I were shooing a cashed roach. Plastic. His eyes, painted and empty, clicking as they shuttered, his lashes stiff polymer. He was a sideshow puppet, a postmodern Pinocchio masquerading in her imagination. I opened his swaddle and checked his drawers to be certain.

Indeed, Chuy was a common doll made in China according to the stamped embossment on his coccyx. I took the bones from my teeth.

"Well I'll be..."

"They are so hot," she said, blowing on her ribs, then biting in, pulling her hand away and shaking it, sucking and blowing air rapidly to cool her tongue.

We destroyed Jack's rack while he watched in mute disbelief from the other room.

"Dude, you got any corn?" she asked.

I had to think about it. I pulled a cold ear from the fridge.

"And some butter?"

I set out the butter and a knife.

"What about mayo? I can't go without no mayo."

I set the jar of mayonnaise on the counter.

"You got salt too? What! Sorry!"

I divorced the salt shaker from the pepper and inched it along.

After licking all her fingers clean she took Chuy back.

"Come, my beautiful son," she said, lifting the final rib to go. "He doesn't want you."

I followed her as she went out the front door. By the time she got to the sidewalk her road bone had been sucked dry and thrown in the gutter.

Jack stood behind me.

"She forgot her sauce," he said.

We watched as they disappeared up the street.

Rap 50

I ONLY WANTED TO SLEEP, AND SLEEP I DID. On the third day I woke from my slumber in the late afternoon. Coffee was next, followed by a squat on the couch. Soon I was in reverie.

The front window was still shattered from when Veronica had requited Mojo months before. The flayed cardboard boxes that covered it had long since fallen into disrepair. They were cracking and bending, rebelling against the duct tape that held them in place. I watched the colors and shadows shimmy through as the sun made its way across the sky. Outside neighbors came and went, airplanes roared from miles above, and unseen sirens wailed the tremors of fragmented lives.

I fished around the ashtray for a butt substantial enough to light. I found a couple of candidates and elected the first. There was a knock at the door. I puffed the first butt down to the filter. The figure at the door began a furious pounding. The screen gonged on its hinges. I lit the second butt.

"Fuckin-a, Mudd!"

It was Veronica. She cupped her hands and peered in.

"I can see you in there. I can see the end of your goddamn cigarette."

"Someone knocks," I said.

"Stop jerking off!"

I sat on the couch and finished the nubby butt before rising. She was out there with arms crossed, smoking two cigarettes. I never failed to marvel at her thoughtfulness. I began to salivate tobacco resin.

"It's about fucking time," she said. "I came by to tell you I'm leaving town."

I stared at her through the screen door.

"Are you gonna open the fucking door?"

I opened the fucking door.

"I'm leaving tonight, moving to Paraguay with a real man."

Just then Francois appeared behind me carrying two suitcases. He was dressed in a seersucker suit and goggled by tinted tortoise shells. A white fedora topped his dome.

"Adieu and merci, companero," he said.

He set the bags down and extended his hand to shake mine. I heard the bones in my fingers crumpling. He undid a bag and handed me a sixpack of La Vitale.

"A sheepment just arrive-ed," he whispered to me. "Et weel save your life."

Then he slapped me on the back. Veronica pulled one of the flaming cigs from her mouth. It was headed my way. My free hand raised to accept.

"Psyche!" she taunted. "Are you fucking kidding me?"

She inserted it between Francois' puckered lips. He promptly smoked it down in two vicious drags, blew the smoke from his nose and spit the smoldering butt on the living room floor. My hand was frozen cigaretteless in mid-reach. When it finally loosened up all I could do was applaud.

"We bought into a co-op on an alpaca ranch," Veronica said.

"In ze heels outside Asuncion."

"I heard it was warm there last year," I said.

"We send a sweatair," Francois said.

He grabbed Veronica by the waist and threw her over his shoulder. Her ass wiggled like two bulldog puppies fighting in a burlap bag, and he could not resist. He snarled and bit one of the pups. She screamed with delight. A taxi pulled up to the curb and honked.

"We go, cheri!" Francois announced, carrying Veronica and the two bags to the curb. He moved as if he were ice skating, smooth and sure. "Adios, companero!"

"Adios, chingon!" Veronica said, flipping me off one final time from the window of the taxi.

As they roared away Francois popped the cork from a bottle of champagne. The cork hit the side of the house and bounced silently into the grass next to the surfboard.

I opened a bottle of La Vitale and sat on the porch. Someone down the street was mowing their lawn in the cool, early evening dusk. The smell of cut grass filled the air with a minty green freshness. I belched softly and said "excuse me" to no one.

I heard a door slam. Nicky came out of his house dragging a bag of golf clubs. I watched as he went to the curb and tipped the clubs into the refuse. Balls scattered and tees rained like shark teeth. He said something I couldn't hear, then kicked the bin on its phalanx to the pavement.

"Take that, golf!" I yelled.

"Fuck that shit!" he screamed. "You know I got fuckin' fired!?"

He stormed over.

"I fuckin' beat my boss so bad on the links he fired me! Fuckin' dog-catchin', ass-grabbin', back-stabbin' bitch!"

He was so grieved his hair was standing up. Veins were popping from his neck.

"That's alright, I took his clubs out the back of his truck when I left."

He looked at me as if I had responded.

"What, you think I'd throw my own sticks away?" he guffawed. "Puhlease! I'm thinking of going pro!"

Gobs of spittle jostled from his jowls.

"Guess I shouldn't have danced on his ass on the back nine!" he mocked. "I buried him! Punk didn't even let me clean out my own desk. Doesn't matter. Got something new lined up. Not even a dog catcher anymore."

He pulled out an envelope full of bank papers.

"I mortgaged my house today, invested everything I have into this business venture..."

He paused.

"...are you ready for this?"

I nodded.

"Are you sure?"

I nodded again.

"Don't lie to me."

"Okay."

"I invested it all in a talking porcelain commode."

I almost nodded.

"It tells guys when to lift the seat."

I looked at him.

"Working with an inventor. I'm capital. Is that not fucking amazing?"

I reached behind me and handed him a bottle of La Vitale.

"What the fuck is this shit?"

"It will save your life."

I sipped my bottle. I felt stronger already.

R.L. Buss has written five books, including *Life Between Cigarettes*, and his fiction, poetry, essays, photos and commentary have appeared in publications such as *San Diego City Beat*, *Happy*, *Impact Press*, *San Diego Free Press* and *the museum of americana*. He once adapted, produced and performed a dramatic reading of Kerouac's *On the Road* accompanied by live jazz. That was pretty fucking cool. *Suspicion of Indifference* is his first novel.

You can view his latest at www.raggedarchetypes.com. He lives outside Chicago.

Ragged Archetypes is a literary and photographic cartel of one concerned with publishing uncouth and brut-folk words and images. Specialties include garage literature, street and geo photography, road poetry, organic journalism, outsider American studies and outlaw ephemera in a geography lacking ads, trends, formulas, pork or pretense.

The cartel is committed to offering books, articles, ideas, images and statements at only the highest levels of creative integrity. This entity believes in the rights and dreams of the artist, not the wallets and contracts of the middlemen.

Ragged Archetypes. Be independent. Do it yourself.

Not in the club.

www.raggedarchetypes.com
muse@raggedarchetypes.com

www.ingramcontent.com/pod-product-compliance
Lightning Source LLC
Chambersburg PA
CBHW020607250626
47154CB00004B/1405

* 9 7 8 0 9 7 1 3 3 6 0 5 6 *